The Professor of Aesthetics

NOVELS BY
CHRISTOPHER T. LELAND

Mean Time

Mrs. Randall

The Book of Marvels

The Professor of Aesthetics

Christopher T. Leland

Z

ZOLAND BOOKS
Cambridge, Massachusetts

FIRST EDITION

Text design by Boskydell Studio
Printed in the United States of America

This book is printed on acid-free paper, and its binding
materials have been chosen for strength and durability.

Library of Congress Cataloging-in-Publication Data
Leland, Christopher T.
The professor of aesthetics / Christopher T. Leland. —
1st ed.
p.   cm.
ISBN 0-944072-37-2
I. Title.
PS3562.E4637P76   1994
813'.54 — dc20   93-38225
CIP

Once again, for Osvaldo

Quel folletto è Gianni Schicchi,
e va rabbioso altrui così conciando

The Professor of Aesthetics

PROLOGUE

YOU WERE October's child.

Not the season of satiety, of harvest, but of the falling days, the ghostly ones more terrible than those of November, December: numb with cold and void of hope. The night of your birth, hope flickered like a fading star at the end of time.

You were born without history: a father unknown, a mother vanished; left in the arms of a woman of embittered loss who wished, cajoled, demanded you call her mother, but for when, in darkness, she touched your chest and belly and sought her true name from your lips, as she spoke yours in a way you never heard in daylight.

You were the furious child wet-nursed, sucking anonymous milk from a hired teat, bruising the soft breast in your hunger for self under the eye of that older woman somber and fascinated. Your home all those years was of perpetual autumn, eternal October, where your presumptive dam played the organ, fussed and dusted, kept you isolate — her possession and prize — deflecting your questions first with a wave of her hand and a glib "When you are older." Later, with tears and a terrified anger, she defeated you even as you grasped her wrist — fragile as an October branch — and screamed for explanation.

Till you tired. Till you could no more and ceased to care, there in that town where from the first you were anomalous: branded in your orphanhood, exiled in your bastardy. Captive of that little house, that dry, frail woman; set apart by your quietness, your eccentricity born of solitude, by your looks different from those of other children — rosy-cheeked and golden-haired — whom you glimpsed through the fence or sat next to in school. These were the ones who mocked you, laughed at your failings or paid you no mind, they of homes complete and established generations upon whom your only vengeance was scornful imitation in your bedroom mirror or, as you aged, imagined judgment upon them by some frightful inquisitor. Their faces you sometimes thought you might have seen in later years, faces which at your very entrance grew paler, broke apart in the whispered, spoken, shouted "No."

You were not ugly: dark-haired, bronze-skinned with eyes a mysterious gray flecked with gold, one with a patch of black so large it made iris and pupil together like a keyhole, the chink through which the moiling within you might have been glimpsed had someone taken the notion to see. But no one did. You were, from the first, too different to be loved. Or the loves proffered were of a kind too rare, too fraught with reasons unknown or unknowable for you as child or man to comprehend.

Yours then was a life always shadowed by fury, the child in you lost to a home prematurely old, its creaks and smells and withered arbor in the garden. Such pleasures as you knew were lonely: the books that transported you; mathematics' cool logic, the feel on your tongue of French, which you learned at private lessons, the only ones you liked among those of music and elocution and dancing. She guarded you jealously, that mother not yours who wished you the epitome of graces, compendium of men: helpful and handsome and bright, but only for her, as if you stood stead for someone never real at all, some creature made of dreams as lost as her potential for joy. You suffered much, but later you thanked her, as your many accomplishments bore you headily through a life of excitement and wealth raised up upon the suffering of others.

A child reared like a ghost, you were always an intimate of death. Despite your attempt in the first moments of freedom, yours was a heart too wounded ever to be shared, one that might attend only to its own desires. So, for you, the unthinkable became commonplace, and even those of your own party looked on you with an awe tinged with despair.

You: angel of darkness, snuffer of hope.

October's child.

I

I CAN'T TELL YOU we weren't surprised. In a place like Christina, we're just not used to gangsters. Why, we wouldn't know a gangster if he sat down to dinner with us, which is what he did, of course, among other things. Jay, I mean. That's what we called him there at the Farrells', like that was his name. "J." is what it said on his card: "J. Skikey, Professor of Aesthetics." How were we to know that was a fake?

Up where he came from they called him Dandy Allan. And he was a dandy, there was no doubt about it. You never saw finer clothes on a man's back. Pretty things. Elegant things. Not sissy or silly looking. The kind of clothes that look like class, that fit just right, that tell you somebody's getting on in the world. He had good jewelry, too. Not that I pay that kind of thing much mind, but you could tell it was real silver or real gold. Not plate. Nothing big or flashy. The way he dressed was like everything about him: smooth, easy.

Like the way he talked — a gentle-man, you'd have thought, and I mean that in the best sense. Seemed like he could sit down and jaw with anybody. And not just in English, from what I could tell, but French and Italian and God knows what else. Now, I can talk plain or I can talk fancy. I can cuss like a sailor or charm birdies from the trees. But Jay, he could talk like nobody I ever met. Except for Callan, of course.

Now if he — Callan McAlpern — if he hadn't been around here, we might've never got wise to old Jay, old J. Skikey, old Dandy Allan. Jay'd've likely stayed on for months, maybe years, who knows? We'd've been rid of him sooner if we'd listened, but, hell, we all figured Callan was jealous. Up to the time Jay showed up, Callan was about the only one around here who knew much about aesthetics. And since he spoke French and Italian too, we thought he probably got his back up when somebody else came to town who could even half keep up with him. Somebody half his age. Somebody who wasn't an undertaker. An undertaker like Callan, anyway.

You have to understand, Callan's a good old squirrel, a good one. Nobody in this whole state would tell you different. But, hell, he's always been an odd duck in these parts. I mean, there he went gallivanting off overseas years before the War — before the local boys went over to do their bit in France: Carmichael Beaupray and Tommy Bob Ellis and Morris Farrell, of course, and the others — but gallivanting off anyways, and then showing up a couple, three years later an undertaker. An undertaker! Well, my oh my.

With old Callan, there's no predicting. He's peculiar, a character, you could say. Not that we don't respect him.

Honest as the day is long and generous, and besides, when it comes down to it, you'd better respect the undertaker!

Anyhow, like I was saying, we're not much for aesthetics and that sort of thing around here, and if it hadn't been for Callan, old Jay Skikey might have been in these parts a lot longer. Of course, he did enough damage while he was here.

Maybe that's not fair. I really can't say what all happened was his fault. But in that week after he left town Edna Farrell lit off for parts unknown and then Morris got hit by the train and, believe what you want, nobody can pretend that was an accident — not to speak ill of the dead. After that, well, Grace Mellors — she's a cousin of theirs — Grace comes down from Missouri to settle the estate and just falls in love with Christina and the house and, before you know it, her and I.J. decide to move on down, lock, stock, and barrel, so I'm out on the streets. No more boarding at Farrells'. I was the last real boarder they had at that house.

Me and Jay Skikey, that is.

◆　　◆　　◆

God treated the Farrells badly. That was what they always said in Christina. Almost from the first, when they arrived from Pennsylvania to set up the shop that would fail in the Depression of 1919, Charles and Edna were scored by bad luck.

The reasons for their migration were never spelled out, though Edna made it a point to affirm from time to time her family's standing in the town she left behind, and her appreciation of life's finer things. The Farrells did have some possessions — glassware and silver and porcelain — that those knowledgeable of such matters said were much to be admired, and Edna had certain airs that seemed appropriate to someone acquainted with greater ease than most women enjoy, but the couple was far from wealthy. It was Charles who knew Christina, having as a young man passed through and worked a spell as a gandy dancer. Enchanted with the hills and the crystalline air — the first of which recalled his roots in the Alleghenies; the second reminding him of what had been lost to the mills and the mines — he returned years later with his wife. There was a common assumption around town that Edna, in choosing Charles, had married beneath her, and that the flight to Christina was as much to escape her family's displeasure as anything else.

Their store was always marginal, redundant in a place with too many merchants already established, ill-stocked for a town that catered mostly to tourists. Charles had no real head for business, a dreamy, gentle man given to tinkering and long, solitary walks through the hills with a flask of rye. With each passing year, he suffered an arthritis more debilitating, while Edna fretted and watched her fine things dwindle with wear and occasional breakage. She was aloof, almost reclusive, and what friendships she maintained in the neighborhood possessed a cool formality that did not set entirely well with the larger community. Their marriage was long childless, to the point there was the usual gossip about separate bedrooms or a variety of female troubles. Then, quite unexpectedly, within two years of one another, a daughter arrived, then a son. After the two births, Edna — a big-boned, heavy woman — wasted through three years of ill-defined ill health, finally succumbing one February before her children could really recall her.

Even on that boy and girl, destiny laid an unjust hand. Little Edna, named for her mother, grew from a spindly child to a gawky young woman of indifferent features and figure. Victim throughout her childhood of underpaid housekeepers either shiftless or dictatorial, then of her father's demands as she grew older and he ever more helpless, she developed a shrewishness the more grating for her youth.

Throughout those years, she proved an undistinguished student, a diffident playmate. She had few friends, and romance or its illusion apparently never sparked her heart. As other girls turned their attention to clothes and boys and the first rituals of courtship, she drew ever further into herself, taking little care with her appearance: never slovenly, but possessed of a frumpish neutrality unnatural in one so young. Beyond her twentieth year, her combativeness dulled a bit as she moved into premature spinsterhood, tending house and store, taking care of her men — father and brother — a figure as distant as her mother before her.

Edna's limitations were all the more notable for Morris. Morris: effortlessly beautiful at five, maintaining his grace even in clumsiest adolescence. Clever and friendly, he disarmed even those who should have disliked him, and retained a goodness of heart his father's indulgence should have spoiled. Over the years, Christina never tired of marveling that Morris and Edna were related at all. Morris: tall and blond, striding through Christina like the young Siegfried himself, the apparent compensation for his sister's homeliness, his father's gradual waning, his mother's early death, for all his family's misfortunes.

Till he went to war. Though wounded, he was not maimed, physically in any case, only scarred a bit here and there, and possessed of a broken tooth he refused to cap. But on his return, he was afflicted with an odd vacancy, a lethargic inwardness that kept him separate from most all life around him. Instead of business or even college, which is where he had talked of going before he put on his uniform, he took a job with the railroad, walking track. When, in the summer after the store had expired, Charles died of influenza, not a few people said it was not the disease that killed him, not even the loss of the business, but the ruination of that final hope that was his son.

Let's see now. I went to board at the Farrells' in 1924, was it? That winter, before Christmas. Of course, I could have stayed on with my sister there at my daddy's house. But I liked Lydia and I liked Tom and they were just married, and I was old enough to know even then that nothing spoils something like that quicker than family underfoot. So, I took myself off to the Farrells, who'd been letting rooms for quite a time, since before the old man died maybe, even before the store went bust, if I remember right. They owned the place clear. Charles had bought it for cash as soon as he came, and it was lucky for them, since even with boarders they barely got by. Edna and Morris, that is. You don't get ahead walking track, which is all Morris was good for after he got back from France.

They'd cut the house up, let the three rooms upstairs. Edna had a bedroom in the back parlor, and Morris fixed up what should have been the pantry to sleep in. Usually, I didn't see him till dinnertime. Slept all day, then he'd come out to eat and head for the station. He'd get back, oh, three-thirty, four o'clock in the morning, after he'd walked from town all the way down to the Junction and back.

Now, Morris Farrell was one strange fellow, when I knew him anyway. I'd seen him back before the War, of course, but he was older than me, oh, a good six or seven years. He was quite the town blade back then, good baseball player and all that. All the girls thought he was a peach, and the boys liked him because he could be a bit of a hellion: sharp as a razor and twice as shiny, as they used to say. He'd get himself in a jam now and then like the other boys, on Hallowe'en and times like that. Nothing serious, you understand, just a boy blowing off a little steam with the best of them.

But that was all before France. Willie Bills says Morris watched Carmichael Beaupray bleed to death there at Belleau Wood. Not that he could have done anything. There was his best friend — well, a friend, anyhow, a boy from home — there in his arms, all shot up and his life just draining away over poor old Morris. That's how he got wounded himself, trying to get Carmichael back where it was safe. Willie says that's what did it, that Morris didn't like the War before, but that after Carmichael got killed, he was never the same. They put him in some hospital over there, and he got better, but then he got worse again and never did see any more action. He came on back and got stranger and stranger, off there in the back of the house.

Poor Edna. Edna about went crazy with him. It was bad enough when the old man was alive. He got pretty cranky, and there toward the end he could hardly walk. But for all the work he cost her, at least Edna could get the time of day out of him. She told me once she thanked God for boarders because that way she got herself a little conversation now and then. She cried. Oh, it was sad. She said to me, she said: "Justus, I can't tell you . . ." Morris went days on end never saying a word but "yes" and "no" and "thank you." Drove her nutty.

So, you can imagine, she liked me. I was no mean catch then. I was working for the county and had a living wage and some good possibilities. And I was around. I was the only permanent boarder they had. Sal Watson rented the room at the end of the hall, but he was gone months at a time, it seemed like, out on the road for American Bolt. The room next to mine was transients: salesmen and widows and somebody's old auntie down for the week that they couldn't stand to have around the house.

But Edna! Well, first off, she was, like they say, an older woman, older than Morris. But I was never prejudiced that way. It's hard enough in this day and age to find a lady you can trust and respect no matter how old she is. But Edna wasn't — I don't want to be mean — well, she wasn't my type, so to speak. A little too prim. Standoffish. The story always went she had a temper that was fierce, though I can't say I ever saw it. A sort of poutiness, maybe. Real chilly.

Then, well, old Jay shows up, and, lo and behold, he starts paying her court. Nothing too forward, but paying attention. A good-looking fellow. Good manners. And hell, with Edna, a girl like that. You know it was bound to turn her head.

◆　◆　◆

Down to the Junction, the walk was easy. Mummer's Mountain — its thick pine forest stopping abruptly just before the summit loomed naked, sheer and black above Christina —

always to his left as he stepped tie to tie down the steep downgrade. In summer, on the longest days, he would reach the switchback as the sun vanished behind the lower, southern slopes, so he trod the gentle falling in the warm, gray dusk. By the time he passed the Horseshoe (not really quite so bent as that) and came to where the track straightened, leveled, and spread easily through the valley toward the river, it was night. In the narrow gorge, lightning bugs starred his path, sometimes almost to the flatness of the levee and the bridge, where the lamp he lit drew legions of mosquitoes and he wished he could strip off his clothes and plunge into the sun-steamed, sluggish water below. From there to the Junction, the walk was flat. In the switchman's house, he would have a bite to eat, with Walter those first years, later with Jed, now with Eddie and his son, Lloyd. Coming back, it was harder from the Horseshoe on, toiling toward Christina, its lights gossamer above the switchback.

It was worse in winter: staggering against the snow, heavy with wool over icy ties with the wind in his face from the moment he entered the ravine. There were shelters on the way where he could stop, but in all the years he had done that only twice, and only after they had told him at the Junction that traffic was blocked farther north, that there would be no limiteds, highballers, milk trains, slow freights through before morning. Mostly, even on the meanest nights, he would stumble into Christina in the predawn's deepest black, so they would know the tracks were clear all the way from the Junction into town.

It was a treacherous route. In the spring and again with the late summer rains, the river might rise within inches of the bridge. Rocks fell from the walls of the valley on occasion, especially at those places they had blasted to widen the gorge. On the switchback, mud slid sometimes during storms, and in winter, there were snowdrifts. It was still all chance, of course. There was no reason why, twenty minutes after Morris Farrell had passed by, a boulder might not shudder loose and tumble across the tracks, blocking the ravine and causing a derailment, a loss of life. But in all the years Morris Farrell had walked track, no mishap had occurred between the Junction and Christina.

At the Junction that night in May, over coffee and largely monosyllabic conversation with Eddie and Lloyd, Morris watched No. 6, the southbound *Bonnie Blue Flag*, thunder by, headed for Christina and eventually New Orleans. It was not quite so proud a train as three years before: shorter, more staid, now more the vehicle of businessmen than holiday travelers on their way to Mardi Gras or to spend a few weeks in Christina, with its certain regional fame as a resort: clean air, fine scenery, good hunting, peace and quiet. Not so many people traveled for pleasure since the Crash. Though few knew it in town, the Hotel Queen Christina on the lower slopes of Mummer's Mountain, built by high-rolling speculators from Hot Springs, was only three months from bankruptcy.

But that knowledge, because of a man in the Pullman *Feliciana Parish,* would never reach the ears of Morris Farrell, who, an hour after the tailgate graced with a single star on a cobalt field was swallowed by the night, began his trek back to Christina.

You were prepared when the moment arrived. Though you had never flown, you had dreamt of wings, of unassisted flight, there on those nights she came to your bed a phantom, somnambulist, her fingers on the nape of your neck and her voice soft against your ear. Speaking your name. But different, as if you were another.

From the first, you turned hard as steel, cold as brass, like some armed projectile that might in any instant launch heavenward away. As it continued, you would squeeze shut your eyes, envisioning another place or time — kingdoms remembered from books, daylight — all to the refrain of that name yours not yours.

Unto the explosion, the fright and confusion you could no longer control, the cry. She would draw back into darkness, sometimes saying: "Dear, did you have a nightmare?" Then came the retreating billow of skirts, and you were alone again in your bed, in your room, awake and determined to flee.

Till that last night. You were barely sixteen, your face still a boy's, but you were decided as one much older. You had gathered all that mattered in a bundle, and certain now that she slept, you pulled your jacket from the coatrack like a human shadow in the black, eased open the window, and slipped — ever so quiet — from the sill to the earth below. You crept along the wall, past the tangled hedge of honeysuckle, out to those October streets cold and hopeless, your own hope dawning with every step brittle on the frostbitten grass carrying you away from that house of eternal autumn into the spring of a world new and unknown.

You did not realize then yours would be a life of flight, major and minor, though it would occur to you later, your face reflected in the window of the El or of a speeding automobile, in the mirror of a Pullman on the *Père Marquette*. Disappearing for a while after the latest crime, you would fleetingly recall that paralysis of your childhood nights, the nausea of hopelessness. Yet you recognized how even that had nourished your will. That was what was important: the will to flee, to do what you wished, what pleased you, that might one day so infuse you that you could commit coolly the mayhem within you. That was what made you a valuable man: an essence the child knew imperfectly if at all, lying exhausted and tearful afterward; one the adolescent alone on the streets of a city far larger and harder than he could conceive would grasp only after falling victim to the will of a man larger and harder but also incautious. From the first time you felt flesh part before your strength, you understood with an electric jolt your own power, your own desire. And you accepted then your fated purpose.

To that you were true, single-mindedly true, in your flight to the South Side, your apprenticeship at the Four Deuces, your first minor assignments in the world of beer trucks and far-flung speakeasies, where you learned Italian — laboriously, secretly: proper Tuscan from a textbook and dialects from those who worked beside you, so no one might deceive you by lapsing suddenly into a foreign tongue. You were officious but not slavish, impressing them with your culture, your wits, and a knowledge of anatomy gleaned from encyclopedias and art books, the odd medical text and an adolescent fascination with the Spanish Inquisition, which, for them, you exploited to obtain what they desired.

You were not famous, notorious; did not boast, in those days, the monikers yours in later years. That is why you were chosen to visit, week to week, Schofield's Flower Shop across from Holy Name Cathedral. You made small talk with the peculiar Irishman there as a soft-spoken and educated customer, so unlike the street-kilned men whom he employed, or those others, their enemies, who were your accomplices. So it was that day, when you entered the store with two torpedoes in tow, that Dion O'Banion, master of the North Side, approached you unarmed, hand extended, and you took it in yours and held it smiling in the rose-rich air. As those flanking you emptied chamber after chamber into the body that danced at the end of your arm, you grasped tighter, yours the very grip of death, proud of the calm you displayed that would win you the respect of Johnny Torrio, of his adjunct, Capone, as they envisioned their rival falling bloody and surprised into fresh lilies and chrysanthemums. When it was done, you leaned over slowly, pressed your pistol to his cheek close as lips for a kiss, and fired.

After that, you fled temporarily, unnecessarily. The Jews and Irish of the North Side blamed Mike Genna for the murder, exterminating him and his sharkskin-suited brothers one by one. Meanwhile, in New York with the Five Points Gang that had groomed your mentors, you refined your particular skills of enforcement upon a series of upstart bosses, stool pigeons, minor merchants and vendors who refused to play by accepted rules or fell behind in their obligations. That was at night. Your afternoons were spent at The Cloisters, before anonymous renditions of Saints Catherine and Bartholomew, Lawrence and Sebastian, patron of archers and pinmakers. In the reading room of the Public Library, you perused Sade in French and nosed through such other arcana as interested you. One evening, in a tiny speakeasy on Broome Street, you told the story — properly expurgated — of your first murder, and your companions teased you with that Italian allusion you would, years later, employ as your alias. After a few months, you moved on to Cleveland, soon back to Chicago, which had new liquidations to contemplate and avenge.

Upon your return, you were much indulged for your talents, and feared, even by those who needed you, for they, though brutal, lacked the peculiar finesse you brought to your arts there in the basement of 2222 Wabash Avenue. From time to time, it was thought wise you be spirited away for a week, a month, though through it all you were lucky: a shadowy figure used infrequently but effectively, improminent on the lists of newspapers and crime commissions, of Hymie Weiss and Bugs Moran. Then history turned, and too, despite your protests, you were forced to be merciful.

So again, you were fleeing, this time indefinitely, from Chicago to Kansas City and on, on to a place where your face or various nicknames evoked no dread, one where you might stay awhile as the Depression-driven son of finer things, your card graced with New York's ironic encomium to your first crime: "J. Skikey: Professor of Aesthetics."

II

Jay was a real pretty boy. Now wait, maybe I'm getting mean on that one. But that first impression Jay made, he looked . . . dramatic, I guess is the word. I saw him that very first night. He'd come in on the *Bonnie Blue*. Along about eleven, the bell rings there at Farrells'. Now, usually, by that time, both Edna and me were long gone to bed, but it was funny that night how we'd stayed up to listen to the radio. It was May and the windows were open and the winter'd been a hard one. Besides, in 'thirty-two, everything seemed a little harder than it probably was. The bell rings, so I go to answer it, figuring it must be some bad news or another. People around here don't come calling at eleven o'clock at night, you know. I open the door and there he is, big as you please and fit for church on Sunday.

He looked like a foreigner, like some people said later, or like a half-breed, if you know what I mean. He had this wavy black hair and dark skin, and a little, thin mustache. He had light-color eyes, I remember, kind of gray. It sounds like it should've looked strange, but it didn't. They sort of jumped out at you from his face. The suit he was wearing cost a hundred dollars if it cost a nickel, the latest thing that was so dark blue it was black, with little stripes through it. I recall thinking then how it shined there in the porch light.

And he says: "Mr. Farrell?"

And I said: "No, no. I'm Justus Bechner, a boarder in this house. And who might you be?"

He just smiled and gave me a card and said: "I was interested in engaging a room."

Now, I had never heard that before, "engage a room." The only kind of engaging I knew about was the kind a man and woman have between courting and marrying. So I told him to hold on, and I turned around to get Edna, who was right behind me anyway by that time. I showed her the card and said to him: "This is Miss Farrell."

He stood real straight and sort of clicked his heels together and nodded his head, real quick, you know. Then he said: "Madam."

Well, you can imagine old Edna. You could see her heart go flutter-flutter, here with this sharp-looking fellow on her porch calling her "Madam" and giving her a little bow. So she said: "Very nice to meet you, Mr. . . . . Skykey."

And he smiled and said his last name, real slow: "Skee-key."

And she invites him right in.

He had one little bag with him. Lord knows what he had inside it. He told us his trunks were down at the station, and sure enough, he had them toted up next day. Anyhow, Edna takes him up and gives him the room next to mine.

When she came back, I said to her: "Well, quite the little slicker, ain't he?"

But she throws me a real mean look and says: "Don't you

worry the man, Justus. We don't get quality people through this house too often. So while Mr. Skikey's here, you mind your manners."

Quality people, I thought. That's a hell of a note. But she was right, of course. Even then, I thought it was kind of funny somebody like him would choose a place like Farrells' instead of a hotel: the Bedford Arms or the Mummer's Mountain Inn. When we found out about him, though, it made sense, since those places were ones where he might run into people from out of town or even from Chicago who would know who he was.

Once I asked him, there in those first couple days. We were out on the porch after supper, and I said to him: "How'd you happen to end up here with us?"

He said big hotels were too noisy and lonely, and he'd gotten the address off the bulletin board at the station, and besides, it seemed better to stay at a place like Farrells' if you were thinking you might settle down for a while somewhere.

And, hell, that seemed good enough reason to me at the time.

◆　◆　◆

He loved the night walk. Regardless of season, it was always black; even in a full moon, the valley was deeply shadowed. The light of his lantern was weak against the loneliness, and inevitably, unconsciously, he found himself fingering the revolver he carried. At night, the hills moved: snakes came out; bobcats padded silent through the brush, leapt up trees, shrieking in surprise, outrage, triumph. Bats whished through the piny air. Only the wild pigs seemed settled after dark. He had had occasion to use the pistol, to frighten if not to kill, and he was happy to have it, though he had loathed guns ever since France.

It was France he thought of, every night, for every feature of that route seemed in the dark not the countryside of his childhood but the land where his entire youth exploded in a few short months. Around the river it was like the place they had first encamped; the ravine, some awful trench for giants, like where he was wounded and Carmichael fell. And finally, as he started uphill, it was like the little town behind the lines where the hospital was, where it had seemed safe and, though still crippled, he was allowed to roam a bit. Where he met Jean Baptiste.

From the first time he walked the route after he took the job, he had sensed those resemblances, and each succeeding trip reinforced them in his mind. With the years, he began to feel the presences, never together: Carmichael's to the mouth of the valley, then Jean Baptiste's at the Horseshoe Curve. He was endlessly patient. The calm repetition of walking track soothed him, and since that moment in France when he learned of the accident, when he realized not the nature of his desires — those he had admitted if not understood — but their terrible and fatal energy, he knew these two, even if dead, could be his only confidants. Eventually, without his urging, they began to speak with him. Jean Baptiste first, later Carmichael, though it was the latter who rested only a few miles away in the Beaupray plot of the Municipal Cemetery. The family had paid to have the body exhumed and returned to Christina. Of Jean Baptiste's tomb he knew nothing at all. Perhaps on a hill by some half-ruined church near Perpignan, some secret Albigensian sanctuary, or, as he would probably have preferred, near the docks in Marseilles, where in his peculiar way he had become a man and learned to drive the trains, where he might hear the switch engines rattling and moaning back and forth beside the piers. But more likely, the body — the scalded, shattered mess of it — lay in the churchyard of Varennes Ste. Claire, unobtrusive, unmourned, the grave of an anonymous outlander.

The two of them delivered to Morris no great secrets of the world beyond. Mostly they soothed his conscience; let him feel their deaths were not somehow his doing. To them, out loud, he would impart what news he had, mostly of Christina and the Junction, of some interest to Carmichael but of little at all, most likely, to Jean Baptiste. He did do some reading, so he talked to them about that, and, for the Frenchman's sake, passed on such gossip as he picked up at the Junction on the latest advances in railroad technology, innovative locomotives on the Delaware & Hudson or the Chesapeake & Ohio.

On that May night, Carmichael was only vaguely present. Jean Baptiste did not make himself felt at all. For Morris, that was not unusual. They came and went from his world as they pleased, and for weeks at a time either or both of them might be absent, going about such other business as might occupy the dead.

The northbound *Belle* thundered past him as he emerged from the valley, right on time. He reached town slightly late that morning, and hardly bothered to do more than shake his boots off before he fell asleep.

◆   ◆   ◆

Well, sir, Jay settled right in: took air out on the veranda and walked his constitutionals through town tipping his hat; had his coffee with us in the A.M. there before I went to work and asked all the right questions. He wanted to know Christina inside out: Who was so-and-so and What was this-that-or-the-other and When this and How that and How much? Oh, he was slick, one slick fellow, I tell you. I only thought of it later, but out there on the porch or over dinner, he never really seemed to have his mind made up about somebody or something until he knew what you thought. Then he'd agree. I remember one afternoon he says to me, he says: "The gentleman at the bank, Mr. Melrose, I believe? He's been in town for some time?" Like that, a question, see? And I said: "Maury Melrose? Five years maybe. No family around here, and with a name like that he's got to be a Jew, don't you think?" "Oh, certainly, certainly," old Jay Skikey says. "Have you had dealings with him?" "Maury, sure. But you got to watch out with Maury. Maury'll take you blind if you don't watch him." "I see. I see."

It only came to me later how he was getting it all out of us, all the information he could. Maury says Jay was interested in real estate. Understand? He really meant to stay here. He'd've probably bought something up on the mountain and who'd've been the wiser? Brought down the boys from Chicago and set himself up real fine. Sent to town for groceries. We've always had a few who did that, rich folks from outside who never had much truck with the rest of us. Come here to fish and hunt and be by themselves.

Oh, he had me taken, I don't deny it. He had me taken sure as he had everybody else. That's probably what brought Callan down there after a week or so. He'd heard tell.

For sure he had. Smack in the middle of a town like this, want to though you might, nobody stays a stranger very long.

But the thing that hits you — the thing that hits me now, even though, back then when it happened, I didn't take all that much notice — was what he did with the Farrells. With the Farrells, it was — and I'm not a swearing man, usually, but — it was the goddamnest thing you ever saw. First, there was Edna. She was in love. In love, I tell you, from the very first day. Now I don't deny it and I'd sure never say it was right, but this town never treated her proper. And here comes this slicker, this shiny crow of a fellow, here comes this fellow who makes nice with her, asks her questions, listens to what she says, and looks on deep, deep into her eyes. Hell, any woman getting a ways beyond marrying age and with no prospects sitting by, well, it's going to make a difference.

If that wasn't enough, you should have been there when Morris met him. Now you'd expect, knowing Morris, that he'd hardly offer up a fare-thee-well to some fellow passing through. I mean, I'd seen it before. We'd had drummers and aunts and uncles and old friends and beaus and belles at that place over the years, and Morris never batted an eye, never said a word, never even seemed to notice there was a strange face at the table. But that night at dinner, the night after Jay got there, well, you'd've thought the angel of the Lord himself had put down amongst us. Old Morris came in, sat down, looked up. And he sat there fish-mouthed. Just wide-eyed wondered in front of old Jay Skikey. He didn't say much — Morris never said much, like I told you, after the War — but he said more that night than I'd ever heard at one sitting. But it wasn't so much that as the look on his face.

I never figured it, but you'd've thought they knew each other. Maybe it was France. Old Jay could have passed for French. Maybe Jay made Morris think about all the high and mighties he'd seen over there in Europe or something. But, Lord in Heaven, you had to be impressed.

◆　◆　◆

He was Jean Baptiste. He was Jean Baptiste come back.

Morris walked down from Christina still unhinged by the vision across Thursday supper, as if Edna and Justus had not been there, as if it were not Christina at all, as if fourteen years had not gone by and he had awakened at Varennes Ste. Claire and, given leave by the surgeon whose own son, they told him, was recently dead, walked down from the château to the village. There, in the Quatre Chats, uniformed and trying out his French on the serving girl, once again explaining his slinged arm and limp, nearing two o'clock, he had first laid eyes on him: short, dark, wavy-haired, cocky in his greasy work clothes.

The place was crowded. They were not that far from the front, so soldiers — whole and maimed — came and went here at the last safe railhead. Beyond, farther into the gouged body of France, there was the danger of shells strayed accidentally or propelled by design from massive German guns, from the odd zeppelin or airplane bombing.

The man came in swaggering, so proud in his coveralls it was a moment before Morris noticed he was lame, his right leg fused somehow so it bent only slightly. He looked different from the others in the bar. It was undefinable. All foreigners, for Morris, possessed a peculiar interchange-ability, so even those soldiers from other regiments on the ship or before the battle were all to him the same sure and defiant other, talking unintelligibly and much too fast. But this man, among the endless Frogs and the odd, mutilated American, stood out. He sat down at one of the tables at the rear, and with startling gray eyes, surveyed the tavern as if he had known it since he was a boy.

Morris, alone with wine and bread at his table, watched as those eyes swept past once, twice, then fixed suddenly on him. The man nodded. When his order arrived, he gathered it up and wove across the room to Morris's table.

"*Bonjour,*" Morris said as he sat down.

"*Bonjour.*" He had a plate full of some pottage heavy with potatoes. "American?"

"*Oui.*" Morris nodded, glad for the conversation. Because of the hospital, most locals had picked up a certain amount of English, the odd word here and there, which, along with his own rudimentary French, was enough to conduct a lim-ited dialogue punctuated by wild circumlocution and charade.

"And how has Ste. Claire treated you so far?"

Morris realized this man could really talk to him. He had learned, in those mere weeks overseas, to recognize the self-confidence that signed that someone was not adrift in the language.

"You speak English?"

"*Oui. Et vous?*"

They both laughed. The man dug into his meal, but never took his eyes away.

"Are you from here?"

"No. No. From Perpignan. In the south."

Morris had heard of the town, hard by the Pyrenees, nestled next to Spain. He had read — innocently — about the whole of France before he had come. He had even talked to Callan McAlpern, who had been in Paris and Nice and Barcelona.

"Where did you learn English?"

"From sailors." The man took a sip of his wine and smiled. "In Narbonne. In Marseilles. I worked on the docks for many years."

He did not look much older than Morris. Morris was bad at judging the ages of these people, who seemed to enjoy no middle years, leaping from youth to decrepitude without transition.

"My name's Morris," he said for lack of anything better, extending his hand.

"I am Jean Baptiste."

His hand was stubby and callused, scarred here and there, dark as the rest of him, but for those surprising eyes. The feel of it made Morris somehow nervous. He pulled back slightly. "You were wounded," he said.

"Twice. First on the Marne." Jean Baptiste smiled bitterly, tapping his knee. "It was this same leg. I recovered in time for Nancy." He shook his head. "Oh, we were very brave. As you were, I imagine. Belleau Wood?"

Morris nodded.

"You lost many friends?"

Carmichael flashed momentarily before his eyes, shattered by the German machine gun. Morris swallowed. "Yes."

"Yes. We have all lost too many friends." It was almost ironic. "You Americans have just begun."

"Now what do you do?" Morris asked, blinking back the

recollection: Carmichael's startled face, and what had gone before.

"I drive the trains." He scraped his bowl clean, and took a long sip of wine. "Sometimes all the way to Paris. Mostly just as far as the junction at St. Juste. Sometimes the other way, too." It was more than a little self-important. "When the line is clear and the shelling is not too bad. Out toward the front."

Morris nodded, exaggerating his respect, though he did respect the man — maimed veteran of two slaughters who still fulfilled his duty, though the Army would have him no more. "Were you an engineer before?"

"They taught me. In Marseilles. On the docks I drove the engines. I was very young." He smiled with the dreaminess of recollections that unshroud only the best. "I ran away. I was sixteen when I left Perpignan. I was in Narbonne and other places and finally Marseilles. In Marseilles, they taught me." He reached over unexpectedly and squeezed Morris's wrist. *"Comprenez-vous?"* he said very softly, then pulled his hand away and laughed. "Cigarette?" He offered a wrinkled cylinder he had obviously rolled himself. Morris accepted. "You are here . . . indefinitely?"

Morris shrugged with his bad arm, a sign it was healing. "Till this gets better."

"We must talk more," said Jean Baptiste, an odd smile playing on his lips. "We will talk some more, Maurice."

"No, no. Morris."

Jean Baptiste shrugged. "Say it how you wish. But Maurice is a fine name. A fine saint. A soldier, like you."

Morris nodded, but suddenly the Quatre Chats seemed close, and this man oddly menacing.

"I have to get back now. To the hospital. To see the doctor."

"Of course." Jean Baptiste stood. "Until soon then." He nodded, almost a little bow, and shook Morris's hand. *"Enchanté, Maurice."*

◆　　◆　　◆

You were a student of faces. The lines and expressions; shapes and deformations. Even in your earliest recollections, it was faces you recalled, though the surrounding scene was now a mystery. What you first sought in them you no longer remembered, though likely it was some unambiguous kindness, compassion, some resemblance perhaps. But the lesson of your life was that the first two had never existed, neither in woman nor in man. As for the last, you no longer cared, self-possessed and self-contained, the man of no history.

Still, you valued faces: slates of the soul and mirrors of the senses. From a face, you made judgments with cool precision — how much trust might be invested; how much respect demanded; how much suffering imposed. You were quick but sure: magisterial observer, serene in yourself as Torquemada, that Spaniard evoked with such fascinated dread in the books dusty on the shelves of your autumnal childhood. By faces you read easily as print, you plotted your life, determined your actions. It was Torrio's eyes that registered his passions; Capone's mouth. That afternoon with Dion O'Banion, you had looked at his forehead, where his hair met skin, to detect any tension. There was none, and you stuck out your hand assured of his innocence, leading him dumb as a lamb unto death.

Here, in Christina, you had known how to respond, sizing up Sammy Pearlman at Western Union the first afternoon, all frights and resentments, which you both stoked and soothed with tales of the larger world outside. You took measure of the banker — Jewish too, but with his roots occluded — and of your fellow boarder. Of Bechner, little struck you: a yokel, a fool, a small-town swell with unrealizable dreams who, nonetheless, like the others, might provide certain information, the lay of the land.

But the siblings bothered you, both brother and sister. There was something queer in that house, hidden and sad. In the faces themselves, something made you afraid, and angry, as if in some other place you had seen them. Was it your presumptive mother in that woman's face, that spinster innkeeper? Did some shadow of the guardian of your days and specter of your nights flicker there, or was it only the etching of solitude across the woman's skin? And the brother? Was it his aloofness that recalled Phelan for you, his mumbling like that rasping whisper of a man who had survived the slashing of his throat? Or perhaps merely their name — Farrell — was enough to connect them with him, its sound and probable Irishness.

The why did not concern you. Your discomfort was excuse enough for hatred, and onto those faces — brother's and sister's — you projected others, those of your victims: Angelos and Davids and Stephans and Toms; Marias, Lucys, and Katies. Time would provide the means of vengeance, as you came to know them, their fantasies and dreads. Your mornings with her, your afternoon saunters to the backyard to engage him: these would supply you the knowledge you needed, what their faces could not speak. At your leisure, you would smash them for the petty irritation, for the vague allusions they made by their very being to those who had made you what you were.

That awareness calmed you. You would not strike from fear or rage. You would do as you wished because that was what you wanted. It was the simple expression of your will.

III

THAT FIRST WEEK or so, things rocked along real nice. It was a pleasure, it really was, there at Farrells' to have somebody new to pass the time with. Jay was the best sort of fellow you could want. He never made you feel small, even though, when I think of the stories he probably had to tell, we must've looked pretty silly. But he never let on, if that's what he thought.

With Jay there, Edna was happy as a sow in mud. Maybe that's not the best way to say it, but you know what I mean. Nice as pie to her, Jay was, and she ate it up. What he saw in her, I don't know. Maybe he figured he could get something off her. Not that way. Necessarily, anyhow. But hell, they did call him Dandy Allan up there, so maybe he was just naturally polite with the ladies. Men like that — sharp fellows who dress nice and all — well, the ladies like them, and Jay was sharp, no two ways about it.

I didn't mean to be out of line there. Nobody can say for sure if anything went on between Jay and Edna. It could've.

I was gone all day and Morris, with Morris you could count on not seeing him till afternoon at the earliest, and he was so inside himself that he could probably have walked smack into the Dance of the Seven Veils and not even noticed. But if Jay needed that kind of thing, like a man does from time to time, well, I set him straight on what Christina had to offer there in the first few days. With the tourists we get through — now, not as many as before the Crash, of course, but there's still a trade — Christina's probably got more in that department than most places this size.

Anyway, I'm not one for gossip and reading in. Jay was good to Edna. He'd ask her what she thought at dinner — and it was a blessing, I can tell you, to have some real talk at the table — and he always called her "Miss Farrell." After we ate, he'd want her to play the piano for us. Edna'd played for years, but I never heard her play so well. I guess I was almost of two minds about it. I was glad to see Edna happy. But maybe I was a little jealous, too. You know how boys are, and much as I liked Jay — and I did, I really did — it kind of got under my skin how much Edna took to him.

Morris didn't have a clue, of course. He just went about his business. I do remember, though, when I came home from work, how I'd see the two of them out back — there was a garden there that Morris would weed and water in the afternoons — Morris and Jay out there jawing, jawing as much as Morris ever did. I went out a couple times, but it seemed then Morris would just clam up. I'm probably making too much of it. Likely old Jay wasn't having much better luck getting Morris out of his shell. Then again, there was that look Morris had around Jay. Hell if I know what they had to say to each other. Maybe old Morris got to practice his French. He'd picked some up over there, I guess.

But like I said, I maybe got a little jealous of how they took to him, the Farrells that is, in spite of the fact that I liked him, too. Maybe that's what made me quick to jump when I ran into Callan McAlpern one day at the Bedford Arms. Couple times a month, I'd eat lunch there. It cost a bit more than I really should have spent. Most days I'd pick up whatever the special was at the Greek's across from the courthouse. But time and again I liked to sit at a table instead of a counter and have a tablecloth and some good silver and a flower in a vase.

There I was, by myself, when all of a sudden who strolls over but Callan McAlpern. Except for Daddy's funeral, which Tom and Lydia did most of the arranging for, I never had too many dealings with Callan. He was older than me, much older, or it seemed like it at the time, and he was the undertaker after all. Anyhow, he walks right up and says to me, "Justus Bechner. What a happy surprise." Now, I really can't imagine he was surprised. He took his lunch at the Bedford all the time, and he had to know I did too now and then. I start to stand up, and he says, "No, no. Do you mind?" And he pulls out the other chair.

He asks after me and my job — and he knew more about everything in the courthouse than you'd figure he would — and then after Lydia and Tom and Tommy Ted, that's my oldest nephew, and my brother Lewis who we hadn't seen hide nor hair of for ten years.

He goes through the whole family and talks a bit about Daddy and was real . . . ingratiating, that's it. He made me feel like he was real interested in just about everything about me. So finally, he gets around to Edna and Morris and, easy as can be, that's got to bring up Jay. When it happened, it didn't even hit me. Now that I look back, I can see how Callan softened me up and then got down to what he wanted to hear about.

I told him what I knew, and the long and short of it is that, before I really caught on to what was happening, I'd invited Callan to dinner at the Farrells'. I wish to hell I could remember exactly how he did it, because, let me tell you, I'd never done that before. I always figured Edna had enough to do, and, besides, she and Morris barely got by anyway, so why bring somebody in for free eats? But there I was, telling him he ought to come by Thursday, that I'd arrange it all with Edna and Morris and how he'd like old Jay, since they could talk all those funny languages and they both knew something about aesthetics. Now there's something I owe to Jay, because that sure wasn't a word I used before he came to town.

Callan told me he'd be honored, "honored" was what he said, no lie, and I should have figured then there'd be fireworks. Anybody who'd be honored to eat at a boardinghouse's got to be up to some devilment. But I still had lots to learn then. Everybody's got learning to do at that age.

He should never have doubted it would come to pass. And confronted with it, with him there in the flesh, Morris felt a strange and terrible relief. He should have known since years before, when the ghost of Jean Baptiste appeared, and certainly from when Carmichael arrived, that he could not escape, that even in Christina, in the womb of all that was familiar, immutable, not to be challenged, it would find him. First spiritual and then corporeal, it would seek him out in the body of a Professor of Aesthetics, who was called Jay Skikey.

Morris smiled, entering the ravine. He did not know what would happen. But he understood whatever was to come was unalterable, determined. From the moment he laid eyes on Jay Skikey, there was no questioning destiny. That he looked like Jean Baptiste — the square of his shoulders, the wavy hair, the light eyes incongruous in all that darkness — still represented no proof of transmigration of either soul or body. But there were those other signs observed in the chats over the pattering watering can: the oblique probing, the right words caressed, the subtle shamelessness of posture, the charged, calm look of evaluation that possessed no single feature but the entire face — the set of the eyebrows, the mouth, the angle of the head. Morris had seen it all in Jean Baptiste. Now, fourteen years after the Frenchman's grisly death, after fourteen years of furious denial in the town of his birth, it had come back to him. And the terror was there, not so much of the thing itself as of what he feared certainly, fatally, it implied. But now, unlike in France, unlike those years when he first walked track, looking back over the ruins of a life dead since the disaster near Varennes Ste. Claire, Morris would accept without complaint what was to come.

Carmichael did not join him in the valley that night, as Morris knew somehow he would not. Unlike ever before, he let himself recall what had happened: not merely his bravery; not merely his loss, but the whole series of events that had sent him wounded in body and terrified in mind to Ste. Claire, from which Jean Baptiste had redeemed him, and from whence he then doubly fled when the melted object of his wantings was brought back from the front.

Carmichael Beaupray should never have gone to war. Carmichael was a sissy. In Christina, in that moment in time, that was perhaps not so bad as it might appear, for in that world, insular despite the tourists who came and went, there was a tolerance as long as one accepted one's assigned part. The strong and weak were sorted out surely as sheep and goats. The strong defended the weak; the weak, when the opportunity allowed or the need arose, defended the order of things, all preparing in their adolescence, after childhood's winnowing, for the necessary relations adulthood would impose in the closed world where each expected to pass the rest of his days.

The War changed that. Before, as if it were scripted, Carmichael read too much, played the violin, joined the debate team and became its captain. He led a serene, virtually monastic life, unbothered for the most part, the fourth of seven children of the Beauprays of Kentucky. The girls he knew were his sisters, those of the string section of the high school orchestra, and Alma Crocker, who was a first-rate public speaker and had announced (to her parents' and the town's mixed amusement and consternation) her intent to become a surgeon. Most people expected, after graduation, that Carmichael would go to seminary, for his people were extremely devout, and then return, if not to Christina to one of the surrounding towns, bespectacled and soft-spoken except for sermons, God's familiar and scourge.

Morris was quite another matter. A middling lineman, but a respectable pitcher and a fine first baseman, brilliant at the plate, Morris was what a young man in Christina ought to be: handsome and clever and innocent. His world admired him easily, happily, and he moved through it aware of his prestige and content with what it brought him: his girlfriend's chaste kiss beneath the elms before his father's house; the shy appreciation of his sportsman's prowess by small boys on sandlots; the sheer pleasure of pleasing those seniors who, in his sixteenth year, took him to the whorehouse one county over, where he climaxed to their applause. Morris hardly noticed Carmichael Beaupray at all in his life as adolescent prince, which required nothing more than beauty and good humor, neither perspicacity nor cunning, exceptional good nor exceptional evil, simply his smile and sheer physical presence, which impressed without relation to gender or age. Charmed, athletic — in theory, Morris seemed made for war, what had been sculpted heroically since the Greeks. War should have made him immortal.

But war is a peculiar and traitorous thing, uncovering unexpected and against our will what we most dread and desire. That was what eventually impressed and terrified Morris about it. The first days after the Easter Week declaration, the prospect of battle seemed merely that of any other game: exciting, a challenge for children bright with the confidence that their simple Americanness would send Germans to rout and so do what French and British boys had failed to do in three long years.

Early in training, Morris had adopted Carmichael, encouraging him, defending him, fulfilling his duty to the natural order as he had been taught. He harangued him through push-ups, clasped his slim waist in those competitions — offering the cheating assistance allowed in a world of men — to lift him through the last chin-up so the next in line might take his place, so their team — red, green, blue — might take the contest. Beneath a fierce southern sun, they all grew accustomed to following instantly, instinctively; to those waves which, one after another, would surge over the lip of the trench and face the machine gun, falling in some balletic, stupid rhythm conceived in Washington, London, Paris; Berlin, the Sublime Porte. When they all had learned that single lesson, when it came as second nature, they were ready. They made the train trip, raised hell in Norfolk, were endlessly seasick. They disembarked and were held behind the lines for weeks. Finally, they moved toward Belleau Wood.

Then they were there. Morris and Carmichael: together and suddenly alone in no-man's-land. Tommy Bob and Willie Bills and the others had pulled back — or they were dead — and the two of them were in a shell hole with fire spewing above them, huddled together: Carmichael and Morris, Morris so scared he could feel the shit inside him pressing to escape. And absurdly, awfully, he wanted it out. He wanted to empty himself of all shit, all breath, all piss, all seed, to blend with the ground in that hole and live.

Morris started to cry. There in that foxhole. There where they thought they were dead. Tears traced through the dirt on his face, sobs shuddering up from his gut. Then Carmichael, ministering Carmichael — silly, sissy captain of the debate team — Carmichael Beaupray pressed against him, put his arm around him, insisting in a shout that amidst the roaring seemed but a whisper: "It's all right it's all right it's all right."

With that touch, confused, with no understanding of the

why, all Morris felt was desire. Weeping against that body, that skinny boy's body destined for the pastorship, he felt it surge inside him, electric and defiant, even to those places it would appall him to admit. He held tighter, and felt against lips dry with panic the stubble of Carmichael's cheek, the crease of his mouth's corner.

Then Carmichael, transfigured with horror or shock or love, with bravery or, perhaps, for once in his life, the determination to prove himself in Morris's eyes, stood up. Stood up, rifle raised, and faced the fire.

An idiot. A perfect idiot. Shattered in a second by some German gunner. There in Morris's arms. Morris who had been filled with want there in a foxhole, now suddenly, unexpectedly with his friend, that sissy, his companion, dying, soaking his shirt with blood — Christina's blood — Carmichael bleeding to death there in his arms, blown apart by lead. Carmichael Beaupray.

Morris gathered him up. There was nothing he could do against that terrible warmth. This was Carmichael, whom he had known since he was capable of knowing, somebody beside him all his life, somebody who, whether he had recognized it or not, was his. So, slick with Carmichael's blood, blood from lungs that could draw no breath, lost to what they were assigned, torn to some hopeless mush that struggled and could not, Morris pulled him from that shell hole, pulled him up and over the earth, not feeling the bullet that splintered his arm, not feeling the other that cleft his thigh and spun him twice in a circle, pulling that body — that body of his friend, the captain of the debate team — over the pocked dirt to the trench, collapsing then, aching for love of that man in his arms who would die within minutes of their arrival at safety.

He fainted almost as soon as he felt the others pulling him down; felt his clothes ripped away from his wounds and the strangling squeeze of the tourniquets, the hands that pried his fingers from Carmichael's body, already cool against his palms.

At Varennes Ste. Claire, they told him that often happened, that — for loss of blood and shock and fear and pain and effort, the courage and strength never before tapped whose release left a man drained — as soon as the moment no longer demanded consciousness, consciousness fled. Of his transport from the front, Morris remembered only the bounce of the ambulance, the gathering quiet, a terrible thirst. Beneath the dull canvas of a field hospital, they probed the bullet from his arm and dressed the hole in his thigh. Then it was into the ambulance again for the silence of the ride to Ste. Claire, to the rambling, frivolous country house of immemorial foundation that had witnessed the festivities, indiscretions, and ennui of generations of aristocrats: Bourbon, Napoleonic, Second Empire, Republican. He woke up finally from the delirium of his wounds and a serious infection, in a ward that had once been a nursery.

Beneath whitewashed walls showing pentimentos of some wallpaper of trees and birds, in glorious, southwestern light that played across the polished floor, Morris reconstructed the moments that had brought him there: despair, desire, the kiss. Other men, those not of Christina perhaps, might simply have dismissed the events; others, again not of Christina, might have embraced them with serenity. But Morris, the prince; Morris, whose life was tied to the town and who had never considered one anywhere else, picked at the memory with the nauseous fascination with which fingers pluck a boil, toy with the festering wound. In that shell hole, something sealed deep within him had been released, and rather than one other mysterious element of his nature, he felt it was poison, something to envenom all his plans.

His strength, day to day, returned, and he took his first steps with a cane. The wound in his thigh had been painful but clean. His arm would take longer to heal for the shards of bone and ravages of the infection, at the height of which they considered amputation at the shoulder. He was anxious for health, but slowed by reflection, so his convalescence lengthened. Finally, to raise his spirits and encourage his body's repair, the surgeon gave permission for visits to Ste. Claire, where, that afternoon at the Quatre Chats, Morris met Jean Baptiste.

◆　　◆　　◆

The first time you touched it, a thrill shot through you from your scalp to your toes. Not that long, but heavy in your hands, you could feel the power in it. They laughed at your excitement, but you were nonplussed, cocky.

"An organ grinder."

" 'Cause it grinds up organs."

"Hell of a lot bigger than any organ you got, sonny."

They laughed again, and so did you.

You had never been given the machine gun before. A pistol; once a shotgun. But on this job — hijacking a truck-load of Canadian whiskey brought down the Lake by a small-time South Sider grown restless and foolish — you graduated to torpedo.

It had not taken long. Only a year and a half before you had left behind that dead place where you had spent your life. It was less than a year since you had fled Phelan's house and presented yourself on Wabash Avenue, the object first of suspicion, even with the information you carried of doings on the North Side. But Angelo trusted you, Fat Angelo of whom at first you were wary, burned by Phelan's initial kindness. Angelo believed your story, though you told only part, and accepted your bruises as proof of assault. You were allowed to stay at the Four Deuces — cleaning up, running errands, sleeping sometimes in the coatroom afternoons. That was where you first met Capone.

He stood over you resplendent as the bodyguard you later knew as Rocco kicked you awake.

"Who the hell are you? Huh! Who the hell!"

The light dazzled you. You could not see, and it was like before: only silhouettes; Phelan pummeling you. You struck back, rabid. Rocco might have killed you had not Angelo arrived.

"He's okay! He's okay!"

"What the hell's he doing here! We don't need nobody sleeping it off in the goddamn coat check!"

"It's okay. He's okay. I can tell you. Come here."

Rocco remained, murderous, as Capone stepped away and you watched with the furious eyes of a cornered dog.

"Lay off him, Rocco." The face loomed over you, the scar slicing it like a mountain range across some distant moon. "It's okay, kid. We don't take to bums around here, that's all. Johnny Torrio don't stand for bums. You want some sleep, you go upstairs to the cribs." He winked. "Don't think there's fun for free up there. Those ladies got business to do later."

From then on, your acceptance grew, you: the willing helper, the apprentice. You met Johnny Torrio, Merlo, the

Gennas, McGurn, and all those others of names not names: Greasy Fingers, Beak, Flat-Top. About your past, you were circumspect, though in a world of orphans and renegades, your heritage was of little moment anyway. You asked questions, discreetly, but most of all you listened, picking up the jargon, pondering the Italian, quizzing Angelo and others as you rolled down midnight streets delivering beer to the outposts of Torrio's speakeasy empire. You came to know the euphemisms, and more important, how the cock of a head or turn of the mouth might speak far more than words. At the Four Deuces, they came to trust you as you came to know them, runners and torpedoes and bosses, the whores upstairs, the jazzbos and dealers in the casino one flight up. You were nearly eighteen years old.

It was different from those first months in Chicago, when three or four times you almost died. Your resources for survival were few, and you feared charity because of the police, who might ship you back from whence you came. It was that possibility, perhaps, that kept you alive those nights the wind blasted off the Lake and you huddled ragged in underpasses and railyards, one more bum — if slightly younger than most — spottily whiskered, thin, locked in combat against the cold. Once, in the deepest chill before dawn, when you kept moving so as not to freeze, as you crossed one of the drawbridges over the river, the water called you to jump. You stood transfixed, tired beyond caring in only those few weeks of battle. A truck passed by, rumbling you back to consciousness. You did not know how long you had stood there, but in those moments of death's seduction, your fingers half-froze to the rail. The skin tore from the flesh as you wrenched your hand away.

You learned first to scavenge, then to steal; partook of fetid slumgullions that ravaged your bowels. Your nose ran; you coughed. You learned to smoke the remnants of stogies and cigarette butts, though you were careful of drink, after a stupor that found you next morning robbed of your coat and gloves, plus two quarters and twelve nickels you had begged the three days previous. All you gained was a headache, dry heaves, and a suspicion of generous companions. You would realize later you had been lucky.

That was only after Phelan betrayed you. You wondered sometimes if he had planned to all along. Otherwise, at that first meeting, he might simply have killed you. He had the gun on you in the junkyard, there where you huddled amidst rags and newspapers in the wrecked Chevrolet. The torch played on your face, a voice whispered through the dark, and for an instant, you thought the last months had only been a dream and you had waked in your bed to the soft sounding of your name. Then you saw the pistol's barrel. Though you later cursed yourself for weakness, your hands went to your face, and you began to cry.

He dragged you out roughly — "You goddamn bums . . ." — and spun you around, the light aimed full in your face — "I ought to . . ."

It was not a shout. It was still that whisper, a growl, a rough croaking. Your fingers dropped from your eyes to see the man.

"Mary's drawers . . ."

You could make out nothing, only a huge shadow darker than the night, some tall, wide, human shape.

"How old are you?" the whisper demanded.

"Sixteen," you said unthinking.

There was a pause. It was January, with a steady, easy

snow. In the light, your nails showed the blue-white of tainted milk.

"Come on."

He pushed you toward the house that faced the street, the junkyard spreading behind it for half a block, plank-fenced against intruders, though you had found the loose board. Inside, it was warm, coal glowing in the stove. A dog lunged toward you as you entered, fangs bared, but a single whistle stilled her. Your rescuer towered over you, ruddy and fat, his gut sprawling over his belt. He held the gun at his side now, and smiled. But what arrested you was the livid swelling running smooth from ear to ear, a wide curve like a second jawbone projected but never installed.

Speeding now up the Gold Coast, you recalled that first night with Phelan, the junkyard, that place you had once thought to call home, mere blocks from those mansions whizzing by on Lake Shore Drive, here in the North Side. The machine gun cradled in your lap, you remembered Phelan's kindness with a sour taste.

"Lucky I found you there. You'd've froze to death in that heap. Or the rats would've got you. Chewed you up while you were still alive." He laughed, handing you some coffee.

The rooms stretched the whole length of the house, and held, you later learned, all that Phelan owned. Upstairs was better junk — furniture and machinery still usable that could be sold intact. Around you were a bed, a sink, a table; chairs and threadbare rugs. At the front door, a cubicle had been built with a counter and a telephone, where Phelan haggled with the public.

Passing into the northern suburbs, you grimaced at your innocence that night, when you still believed in salvation.

You had sipped the coffee, and smiled at the man, warm with gratitude. Afterward, you slept on a mattress on the floor, racked suddenly by fever, your body, after such protracted struggle, collapsing in the first instant of comfort. For two days, you hovered near delirium. Phelan nursed you, and once again you felt indebted, a sense that would grow foolishly into trust and a peculiar affection as your strength returned and you labored amidst the junk, coming to know both Phelan and his business.

He was a man in his middling forties, an Irishman brought as a child to the North Side, where he had since remained, already immense and going quickly to fat. He ate hugely and drank more, and half a dozen times in your stay there, he vanished for hours into the night, to return at three or four, apparently sated, royally drunk, ready for sleep. His throat's condition was the result of various accidents or assaults, depending on his mood: a cable had snapped in a mill where he worked and beheaded three others before mangling him; one of his own brothers had tried to murder him with a razor in his crib; a gang of thieves had robbed him in an alley and left him for dead. You believed all the stories and none at the time. Later, the truth did not concern you. You only wished who or whatever had attacked Phelan had done the job more thoroughly.

You came to know him well enough to conjecture the most likely explanation. Many nights, Phelan threw open the gates of the yard for trucks that, hidden by mountains of castoffs, sat all day to be reclaimed next evening or the next by gruff, hard-faced young men of the kind you would later become. You had learned enough in a pair of months on Chicago streets of the trade in liquor and the rivalries

that existed among those so engaged. You suspected someone on the South Side was responsible for Phelan's whisper,
for he loathed all those from beyond Division Street. The
men who appeared in the night at his junkyard were Irish-
men — "All Paddys and a couple Polacks, with a Jew or
two thrown in," Phelan would say, often as prelude to a
curse on Italians, "Whoremongers and pimps. Yodelers and
cowards." Perhaps his house and job were a reward for
services that had left him all but mute, for he was often
cavalier with those who brought the trucks, agreeing to
receive them or not arbitrarily. Lunging for the jangling
phone in the early morning darkness, he would respond with
nothing more than "Okay" or "Not tonight." If the first,
he dressed and waited for the brief bleat of a horn, then
lumbered outdoors to let in the truck. Though sometimes
you peeked through the window, you always waited inside.

You were waiting now, in the car amidst the trees: you
and Flat-Top and Tonyo and Angelo. They would have to
come this way, down this leafy, suburban road, having fer-
ried the whiskey to the beach and loaded it onto the truck.
The point of this raid was not the liquor, not the money it
could bring. Angelo had told you: Johnny Torrio made more
in a day than the whiskey was worth. The point was dis-
cipline. Had Scrimaglio asked, Torrio would have permitted
him to bring in the shipment, for a cut or perhaps not, for
Torrio was a reasonable man, willing to make allowances
so business might continue with a minimum of bother. But
Capone insisted, Angelo had told you, and Torrio agreed.
Scrimaglio had grown greedy, had only a small following,
and, worst, had sought counsel from O'Banion, a man the
South Side held in ever greater suspicion.

Angelo checked his watch, revving the motor, and kept his window open despite the cold. You, in the backseat on the right, stroked your tommy gun, restless. A few cars had passed in the last half hour. There had been no conversation, only the brittle silence of the winter's night.

Then, unmistakably, came the laboring of a truck, a dull moaning and grinding of gears. It pounded by suddenly, gathering speed.

"Hit it!" Tonyo barked, and Angelo slammed the car into motion as a blue sedan, Scrimaglio's car, shot by.

"Make it fast!"

Angelo accelerated steadily, then shifted, cutting sharply into the other lane, clipping the distance second to second that separated you from the sedan, trapping it behind the slow-moving truck.

"Get ready, kid," Angelo shouted, but your window was already open, the wind surging in your face, your hair, your slitted eyes. The barrel of your gun rode the frame, and you waited only for those last feet to evaporate.

"Now!"

Your finger slammed onto the trigger, and the gun butt danced against you as the car swept abreast and past the blue sedan. Your bullets chattered for mere seconds, but now — as out of the corner of your eye you saw the tailgate of the truck — the sedan's headlights veered sharply right and down, skipping over the embankment beside the road. You heard the muffled crash as it struck a tree.

"Careful of the driver!" It was Angelo again. "We want the truck!"

The car drew up to the cab now. Tonyo pulled out his revolver. As you readied for a second sweep with the tommy gun, you heard a single report, so sudden you did not know what had happened. The truck was slowing. It rolled gradually to a halt as Angelo braked. One door opened, and the driver jumped out, bleeding badly from the shoulder.

"Careful! He's got somebody riding shotgun. Rake it!"

As the car swerved in front of the truck, you leaned out again and fired a burst that shattered the windshield.

"Bring your goggles, Flat-Top?" Angelo asked casually.

The man beside you, stoic throughout, only nodded.

Angelo stopped the car, and Tonyo threw his door open, rolling along the macadam and down the embankment, out of the truck's headlights. As you did the same, you saw him already running. He wrenched open the passenger door. Stumbling to your feet, you saw a dark shape from within the cab fall limp to the pavement.

By the time you reached his side, Tonyo had brought the driver around, forcing him at gunpoint down the lip of the shoulder into the black. In spite of the night, you could see a spreading stain on the man's shirt. He was gibbering, a kind of keen. Perhaps, you thought, he was praying.

Angelo had turned the car around and waited above.

Tonyo slapped your shoulder. "He's all yours, kid."

Then he walked away.

You stood half a dozen paces from the driver. He was not much older than you, but taller and heavier, and fair, as best you could tell in the starlight and weak penumbra of the truck's lights still aglow on the road. Rather like Phelan when he was young, you supposed.

"Please don't please don't please don't . . ."

You listened. Was there a brogue to it, the slightest suggestion? The man was weakening, loss of blood robbing him of breath, his words fading to the merest whisper in the darkness: soft, unintelligible, sexless.

Your finger only twitched. At that distance, there was no need for more. Standing over the body, you fired again, briefly.

You pursed your lips, and tasted blood.

"Hey!"

You climbed back to Tonyo and the others. Flat-Top now held the wheel in the truck. Angelo grasped a trussed figure by the collar.

"Scrimaglio," he said as you approached. "Lucky for us. Capone wanted him in one piece."

The man's face was cut.

"He okay?"

"Glass." Angelo shrugged. "You can help me keep an eye on this joker on the way in. Tonyo's riding with Flat-Top."

You heard the door slam, and the truck pulled away. Angelo shoved Scrimaglio into the trunk of the car.

"Let's go."

On the way into the city, Angelo praised you. You basked in the approval of the fat Italian, but deep within, it was only your pleasure that concerned you. You would not judge yourself on others' terms, not Angelo's, or Tonyo's, or Capone's. Not even Johnny Torrio's himself.

"What do we do with Scrimaglio now?" you asked.

"Don't know" — Angelo was vaguely guarded — "probably take him downstairs. Capone'll want that."

"What'll Torrio want?"

"He lets Capone take care of that kind of thing. You ever been downstairs?"

It was the first time you had heard of the cellar at the Four Deuces. That night, you were not invited there.

IV

I SHOULD HAVE known it would be a bad night. I should
have figured it. But I was pretty stuck on myself, I guess,
and here was Callan McAlpern showing me what a comer
he thought I was — I told myself that, anyhow — and him
and old Jay would hit it off real fine, to my mind, and that
couldn't be bad for me.

Edna wasn't the problem you might have thought. She
sort of liked the idea of somebody else new at the table,
especially Callan, because I guess she thought he was quality
people, too. She oven-roasted a hen that night, with bread
and walnut stuffing, and made the orange peel relish she
usually did only on Sundays.

When I told Jay, he seemed happy enough, but he was no
easy fellow to read. Probably he was suspicious of anybody
who wanted to meet him, especially somebody who was,
you know, cultivated like him. But he didn't let on. Acted
real pleased and said it would be nice to get to meet someone
he'd heard tell about in town.

Nobody said anything to Morris, of course. Maybe Edna

did, but I doubt it, and I figured there wasn't much point. Like I told you, old Morris didn't give two hoots about most things. That's why him being impressed with Jay was so funny. For years and years, there'd been different folks around that table, and after somebody'd moved on, it'd take Morris a couple, three days to even notice he'd gone. He was off in his little world walking track, and there was no reason to think he'd care less about Callan McAlpern showing up for dinner.

Sal Watson was through that week for a couple days, back from his southern swing, ready to make his western one that would take him all the way to the Coast sometimes. I asked him if he was going to be around for the get-together coming up, but he was due in Joplin that night, but said he was sorry to miss it. Then, he gave me this funny smile, like he knew somehow things might get sticky. He didn't have much truck with Jay while he was there, and not really much with the Farrells either: paid his rent and used his room. Half the time when he was in town, he didn't take his meals there. Just clanked around with his display case and a few loose bolts in his pocket. The two of us would chat now and then, but really, after only a couple weeks, I maybe felt closer to Jay Skikey than I did to Sal.

Funny now to look back on it, since it turned out that what we really knew about Jay didn't amount to a hill of beans. And it was that night, though we didn't realize it at the time, that the person we thought Jay Skikey was started to come apart.

Callan came by about five. By then, it was summery, so he had on this white suit and a fine gray tie, with a rosebud in his buttonhole and his arms full of presents. He had a bouquet of carnations for Edna and a bottle of peach brandy so we could all have a nip before grace. With Callan, you'd've never known there was Prohibition. He always had a stock of hooch up there at the parlor, along with such a collection of geegaws from hell and back as you've never seen.

Anyhow, he also brought something for each of us, wrapped up like Christmas, pretty as you please, even something for old Jay. Edna takes them and says she'll put them on the table and we can open them up at dessert time, like we each one was having a birthday. She was tickled, she was. And, you know, I wondered then how long it had been since anybody gave her flowers, or if anybody ever had.

About that time, Jay came downstairs, and Edna said she had to get things ready in the kitchen while we gentlemen got acquainted — "gentlemen" was what she said, which was sure the first time she'd ever called me one — and she told me to get the cut crystal glasses in the parlor. Now those glasses her mother had brought down from Pennsylvania, and, I swear to you, in the whole time I'd lived there, I'd never seen them anyplace but in the china cabinet. So I introduced Jay and Callan and went to get the glasses, and just that quick, when I got back, I got this feeling things weren't going to go real good.

We went out on the porch. I felt kind of silly out there in public and everything with that sissy glass, but neither one of them seemed to mind much, and I was trying real hard to be classy like they were. But they probably wouldn't've noticed if we'd gotten arrested for violating the Volstead. No, they were too busy sizing each other up. You know how dogs are? How they circle and act like they're looking away, but they're keeping a good eye on each other, sniffing the air, and they'll growl a bit, quiet down by the belly some-place, each one saying to the other he better mind who he's talking to? That's what it was like when I came back. You could smell it like you can smell it before a dogfight. Old Jay and old Callan weren't going to hit it off at all.

Now, they were both too polite to just call the other one a son of a gun and go after him. I don't know if Callan would have been so brave if he knew then who Jay really was. From what we heard later, Dandy Allan or whatever you want to call him was one cold-blooded fellow, killed people and worse. But we didn't have a clue. Callan just thought he was a phony; fancy clothes and snake oil, and Jay figured this was probably the one person in town who could make things hot for him.

But from what they were saying, why, they were nice as pie. Callan kept parading all his fancy words, but Jay under-stood, I guess, and he'd say some whole sentence in French and Callan would answer him and then they'd look at each other with those kind of nasty grins that mean "I'll get you next time, you so-and-so." It got so bad I finally said: "Look, fellows, I think it's swell you can yammer six ways from Sunday, but I'm a country boy and faster than a preacher's son loses . . ." Well, you know what I mean.

They both laughed and said they were sorry and then Jay said: "Mr. McAlpern just wants to make sure I'm an honest man." And Callan smiled. Cocked his head and smiled, and then Edna came out and told us dinner was ready.

We went inside, and, I can tell you, Edna'd laid out quite a spread: done yams and rolls, not biscuits, and she'd put the rest of the walnuts from the stuffing in with the string beans. Somewhere, she'd found some candle holders. I guess those were her mama's too probably, and we'd never in all my time there had dinner by candlelight. Maybe they did it on holidays when I was over at Lydia's, but I doubt it.

So there we all were, and in comes Morris. Even he looked surprised with all the fuss Edna'd gone to, and he was probably even more surprised to see old Callan there. Callan slipped over like they'd been buddies since Hector was a pup and says: "Well, Morris, how have you been? It's been a long time." And Morris eyed him like, yep, it had been so long he couldn't even remember when the last time was.

Maybe there was more to it than that. Maybe Morris had it figured what was going to happen, and he was already on Jay's side. It wasn't that him and Callan had ever had much to do with each other. I guess they'd talked some. Edna told me once, I think, that Morris'd gone over to Callan's before he went to war, seeing as how Callan had been to Europe and was the only one in town who really knew much about France. Anyhow, Morris gives him this funny look, and then we all sat down and Edna said grace and we dug in.

It was a hell of a meal. I don't think in all the time I was there, I ever ate better. But I couldn't enjoy it like I should've, because that meanness between Jay and Callan was too thick to ignore. I thought maybe I was the only one who noticed, but it was clear soon enough that Edna'd picked up on it, and even Morris.

Like I said before, it wasn't really what they said, just how they said it, and the way they looked at each other. It wasn't hate exactly. It was, well, I guess the way Jesus must have looked at Judas at the Last Supper when he talked about being betrayed. They flipped all those big words back and forth and they'd say things in French and Italian and Latin — I got a little steamed, I can tell you, since I'd already mentioned it once, but you'd've thought Morris and Edna and me weren't even there — and there comes a point where Callan says: "Seems you're very interested in Christina, Mr. Skikey." And old Jay says: "Indeed, Mr. McAlpern." So, Callan says something about it was odd that somebody of Jay's — what was it? — erudition, somebody of Jay's erudition would settle in a place like Christina. And old Jay chuckled, you know, that "heh-heh," and says that if a man as erudite as Callan had come back to be undertaker here, the town must have a lot to recommend it. I can't do it justice. It was funny in a mean way and I got tickled by it. Probably I was nervous and it hit me right, but I laughed, and then, just think of it, Morris started to laugh too, so finally Edna had to crack a smile.

Well, that was the beginning of the end, because Callan McAlpern does not and never did take to anybody making a joke out of him or him coming back or him being an undertaker. So he smiled, too — but you just knew he was mad — and says real easy: "Oh, I've been meaning to ask you, Mr. Skikey, about your name."

By that time, Edna was clearing the table. There we were: candlelight and our dessert plates and the peach brandy bottle on the sideboard, with those wrapped-up presents for each of us from Callan sitting there. You could see Jay'd been expecting that one somehow, like he'd figured Callan'd bring it up from the first time he saw him. But it spooked him. He took a slug out of his water glass, and then he said: "Yes."

"Now, you spell you name S-K-I-K-E-Y?"

"That's right, Mr. McAlpern."

"Is that a Polish name? Or Bohemian? Or something invented like — "

Then Jay interrupted and said: "It's an Italian name, Mr. McAlpern, as I think you know."

Edna brought the pie in. It was an apple and cherry one with a crumb topping she'd invented all by herself, and it was about the best pie you ever ate. While she was serving, I made lots of noise about it, about what a lucky bunch of fellows we were and sweet-talking Edna about all the trouble she'd gone to, hoping maybe Jay and Callan would let things drop.

Callan wouldn't. Callan's a little man, short, I mean, and he's like a terrier. You know the type. Feisty. They can't just go for the kill. They fret whatever they're after, worry it so bad that it gets tired, and then they go for the throat.

But Jay was no easy prey, mind. Being the out-of-towner and all, he was playing real nice, but he wasn't going to let Callan get his goat. Edna gives us all coffee and brews herself a cup of tea with some tea egg I never saw before either. She must've raided every barrel and crate squirreled all over that house.

Now, Callan says, like there'd never been any interruption at all: "But, Mr. Skikey, there are no *k*'s in Italian."

Jay just smiled, but tight, you know, and he says: "You may know that, Mr. McAlpern, and I know that, but immigration officers did not have the privileges you and I have enjoyed."

Well, I thought Jay'd taken that round, too, but Callan sips his coffee and says: "So, it is Schicchi?" I can't do the pronunciation right, but he says it different than Skikey.

"And the J., I suppose, is for Johnny? Or Gianni?" That time again, it was the same word, but different, rolled different.

Jay took out his cigarettes. He was nervous. There was no mistaking it. But he was going to humor Callan, tell him what he wanted to hear. He said: "As you wish, Mr. McAlpern."

"Johnny Skikey," Callan said, and then (you've got to suffer me here; I can't do it justice), "Gianni Schicchi!"

It was loud, like he'd just struck oil. Then, under his breath almost, he said something else. In Italian. Sounded more like that than French to me. And Jay sat there looking like he could have killed Callan on the spot.

The funny thing, though, was Morris. He had a face I'd never seen before, like he couldn't take much more of the whole business.

So Callan says: "Well, Mr. Skikey, I can only say your father must not have — "

"I never knew my father, Mr. McAlpern."

"Well, then, I — "

"He died before I was born — "

"Well, it seems that — "

Then, no lie now, Morris of all people pipes up and says: "That'll do, Callan."

Not loud. You know how people can say things soft they might as well bellow? You've got to remember that ninety-nine percent of the time, Morris never said a thing at supper. But that night, there he was looking at Callan McAlpern and, when you come down to it, telling him to shut his mouth.

And Callan starts out: "I just meant to say that — "

Morris folds his arms then and says: "I said, that'll do, Callan."

Callan looked at him and — I don't know how to explain it, because I never figured it — but he looked at him with one of those wiseass, pardon, one of those looks that says, "Oh-ho, I see what this is all about." Morris picked up on it. It was in his face, something scared, but then he got his easiness back.

And Callan says: "Of course, Morris."

He finished up his coffee and pulled out his watch and, my, oh my, where had the time gone and he had things to do and wasn't Morris going to be late for work?

Edna said — poor Edna, she was just sad things hadn't gone better, and you could understand with all the trouble she'd gone to — Edna said: "Now, Callan, don't you run off before we've had a chance to thank you for these lovely gifts."

But Callan said, oh, no, that it was embarrassing to have your presents opened in front of you, that he hated it, and he really did have to get himself home. So we stood up and shook hands all around, except Callan kissed Edna's, and even him and Jay made out like they were bosom buddies and they'd have to see each other real soon and Callan said he'd show himself out.

We sat there, and we heard the door close, and it was real hard, especially for me because I felt it was all my fault somehow, how Callan and Jay hadn't gotten on and all the work Edna'd put in. We're all sitting there, and Morris — now, Morris, mind you — Morris reached out and picked up his present and tore off the paper. Callan had given him a scarf, a nice wool one for winter, and Morris says: "Well,

Callan never gave somebody something he didn't think about, I guess."

We laughed then. I don't know why, maybe because we were all trying to make it seem like everything was really all right. So Edna opened hers, which was a pearl stickpin, a fine piece, even I could see that, and I don't know a damn about jewelry. My present was five Havanas. I don't smoke much, but I love a good cigar when I'm in the mood, and I'll hand it to Callan, he was no fool about how to win you over.

Then it was Jay's turn. He unwraps his package real carefully, takes his time. It was a book, an old one, maybe even one Callan had picked up when he was in Europe, which had been, what, thirty years or so? It had some other man's name written in front, inside. It was all leather and had the title in gold down the back and on the cover.

Jay turned it over and over and kind of smiled, and then he said: "Where he wishes I were, I suppose."

It was a copy of the *Inferno*. In Italian.

Many years had passed since he had recalled it so completely; had allowed himself or been allowed by those ghosts who joined him there on his nightly round. But once the memory of Carmichael returned, he knew too that of Jean Baptiste would demand a hearing. His eyes still red from the moment when he had had to stop there along the tracks, sob in the darkness for the lost boy whose body rested a few miles away, he recognized as he lay in bed in the black slowly turning to dawn that to recollect Jean Baptiste would be even more hurtful. But even then he felt an exhilaration he had not felt since the War, a thrill before the abandonment of the mundane for the extraordinary. Something about Jay Skikey — was he the only one who felt it? — made life immediate for Morris in a way it had not been since Varennes Ste. Claire, since the death of Jean Baptiste.

The doctor had encouraged him to go to town. In the afternoons, Morris felt almost duty bound to take the short walk through the grounds and down the hill, convinced by those at the hospital the summer air and the exertion and the at least vague normalcy of village life were as essential to his convalescence as anything else. So it was that he saw more and more of Jean Baptiste. Sometimes they would share lunch; sometimes he would encounter him on the street; occasionally the Frenchman appeared in the late afternoon at the Quatre Chats and Morris would drink more wine than he was supposed to, getting drowsy in the warm light as Jean Baptiste talked of Perpignan and Marseilles and driving trains.

One day, Morris arrived early and walked down to the station. Jean Baptiste called to him from the cab of one of the wheezing engines assigned to the sector. Morris knew nothing about steam power, but the machine looked ancient to him, decrepit, even dangerous. Various parts of it — pipes, even one of the drive shafts — seemed improvised, jerry-built. He mentioned it to Jean Baptiste, a bit abashed, for he had never seen his friend cockier, more swaggering in spite of his limp than at that moment, the oil on him still shimmering, certain with his engine.

"Oh, it is true," he said ruefully, "the run to St. Juste is not that important. There you see fine machines. But from here towards the front, why risk a new engine? The danger isn't that great, but it happens. A shell blows out a section of track. There have even been some trains hit."

He shrugged. It was something Morris had learned to admire, grudgingly, about Europeans, about the French anyway, certainly about Jean Baptiste: that fatalism that allowed them to face the grimmest eventuality with terrific equanimity, as if disasters were brought on not by miscalculation or shoddy maintenance but destiny.

"At St. Juste," he was saying, "at St. Juste, there are 231s, and Atlantics."

It was almost reverent, his pleasure in the machines, those he likely had never had the chance to drive, ones they would not have used on the docks at Marseilles, ones which, from the cab of a silly switcher, that runaway boy must have admired: massive Pacifics roaring north to Paris with the exotic plunder of Algeria, Morocco, Tunisia.

Morris had never quite understood what Jean Baptiste's life had been like there in the south, after he orphaned himself. At seventeen, he had been an engineer, at least that's what he said, and the intensity of his pride in that moved Morris, seemed oddly innocent, as if Jean Baptiste, in spite of the Marne and Nancy, were still a boy, still almost sensually atingle with the power of those machines, as if that somehow saved him from the horror of what he had witnessed as a man.

For Morris, that was attractive, hypnotic, because he felt himself old as those engines at Ste. Claire for what he had been through. To see Jean Baptiste — energetic, so full of joy you did not notice his limp — was the proof it was possible not only to survive but prosper, survive and regain or retain that innocence, be that boy golden with possibility in spite of the trenches and bullets and Carmichael Beaupray. Perhaps, he later reflected, Jean Baptiste had recognized his vulnerability and exploited it. But he did not believe that. It would be too painful to believe that.

After a tour of the train yard, they did not go to the Quatre Chats but to a bar — hardly a place at all — for a bottle of wine and more talk. They argued and laughed and touched back and forth as their jokes grew more complicated and the alcohol ran through their veins, touched more than Morris was used to touching: the hand to the shoulders, the fingers grasping the forearm for emphasis. But this was France, after all, and the world at large a different place from Christina.

Finally, dusk was falling, and Morris knew he was drunk.

"I've got to get back now. The doc'll kill me. Jesus." He laughed. "I've had too much and it's late and they'll kill me."

Jean Baptiste took him by the arm, and they went out to the street, up through the town toward the lane that led back to the château. They were just beyond the gate when Jean Baptiste veered off the road. "This way. It is faster."

Through the woods in that blue hour after the sun has set but night has not yet come, in through the trees, Morris felt utterly lost, his head light from the wine, the evening chill passing through him, with nothing in any direction but the order of the planted forest, trunk after trunk in infinite file. Jean Baptiste took his hand, led him farther into the gloom. Morris giggled, alcohol settling over him in a billowing cloud.

Suddenly, Jean Baptiste turned. Morris felt his breath in

his face, then his lips, his tongue, those stocky engineer's arms on his back. He was weak, all his wind fleeing him before he realized what had happened, straightening sharply, pulling back.

There was a hand in his crotch, and a mocking, playful voice said: "Whistle! Whistle!"

He began to laugh, and in spite of that hand grinding there where he knew it had no right to be, he kept trying to pucker his lips — "Whistle!" — which was impossible because it tickled and was funny somehow and, ultimately, he did not mind it for the drunkenness or something else.

Then the fingers went away, and he tumbled back in a way that would have hurt were it not for the wine.

Jean Baptiste helped him up. They were in a clearing, from which a muddy path led toward vague lights.

"There is the château," Jean Baptiste said. "You will meet me here tomorrow?"

"Tomorrow?"

"Tomorrow I do not work. I will wait for you. At noon."

Morris shook his head to clear it. "Sure. Sure. Tomorrow." He looked up the path. "That's the castle?"

Jean Baptiste nodded. He took Morris's hand and slowly, almost ceremonially, raised it to his face. He pressed his mouth against the flesh of the heel, that mound below the thumb, his teeth closing gently, pulling the skin and muscle together, releasing it before it had a chance to hurt.

"I will wait for you, Maurice."

Next morning, the dregs of the previous evening pounded through his temples like regiments at drill. The doctor looked in as, to exercise his arm, Morris squeezed again and again an alabaster egg. He made no mention of his patient's lateness the previous night, though he did remark dryly that Morris seemed to be recovering well, and that perhaps time spent walking the surrounding country rather than sedentary in Ste. Claire would be more salutary. Morris agreed sheepishly, adding that today he planned to stay at the château.

And that was his plan. From the moment he awakened hung over from the cheap wine, what had happened in the clearing chilled and angered him. What had he been taken for? Who was the monkey-suited Frog who'd grown up on the docks — staying alive God knew how — to take advantage of him, drunk and wounded, kiss him and touch his privates? The next time he saw him, he would ignore him, expose him, punch him in the mouth — those stubble-framed lips he had felt against his own — to show him exactly what he thought of French degenerates and dock rats.

He settled on that course over breakfast, but later, as he sweated from the exertion and dull pain of the repetitive therapies — the hurt possessed of an odd voluptuousness as it signaled his strength growing infinitesimally day to day — his emotions softened. Perhaps it had all been a game, and even if not, Jean Baptiste, who it seemed had grown like Topsy in a world of no codes or compassion, could not be blamed for who he was. Morris, like all boys, had had those moments when curiosity and ignorance or the unaccustomed and undirected lust of adolescence led dangerously close to forbidden paths. It had come upon him amid locker-room braggadocio or teenage roughhousing or . . .

His breath caught in the midst of lifting the five-pound weight with his elbow resting on the table. His eyes misted.

"Does it hurt too much?" The nurse steadied his hand. He blinked.

. . . or in the moment of presumed death when there is only the wish to affirm joy and love one final time.

"No. No. I just thought of something."

"Well, that should be enough for today."

She was pretty, and always kind to him. Millie, from Colorado. She smiled shyly.

"Are you going to Ste. Claire today?"

"No. I think I'll read."

"Well," she said from the door, shaking her finger in mock severity, "if you do, don't let those Frenchmen corrupt you."

He knew it was a joke, but his eyes must have betrayed the panic that washed over him cold and sudden as a wave. Millie stopped, perplexed, then smiled.

"Don't worry. The doctor wasn't mad about how late you were. He said it showed how much better you were feeling."

In any case, he would not go today to the rendezvous arranged against his will. He would read, or talk with some of the other wounded in the ward: Lansdowne from Kansas or Micheletti from New York. Or he would go downstairs to play poker or rummy. Perhaps Millie might even have some time. They could sit on the terrace and watch the sunset while she told him about the Rockies and he told her about Christina and his father and Edna.

All these possibilities emerged, crowded one another out, appeared reborn in combination and permutation as he sat three-quarters dressed in the ward and the clock above the doorway ticked toward twelve.

He could hear the chimes on the town hall, sweet through the lazy, June stickiness, as he hiked — his leg today as if it were as good as new — down the lane, veering off on the narrow path he had never really noticed till the previous night, casting one unnerved glance behind him before slipping into the cool gray that would hide him from any casual observers. His steps were muffled by the cushion of the rooty forest floor, his head somehow lightened by the damp smell of earth. He emerged into the clearing. Around him, there were numerous stumps and a fallen tree covered with vines, here and there a clump of wildflowers. There was no sign of anyone. He sat down on the log to wait.

There was no honest explanation of why he had come. No logical one. Something stronger than outrage had brought him. Even in his innocence — which despite the War remained great within him; which he brought from Christina; which he planned to take back with him intact — he realized he was being drawn in directions that frightened and seduced him simultaneously. And that admission brought unbidden recollections immured or forgot, the images caught by eyes that wandered or lingered too long at the pond, in the showers, at some unexpected instance of nakedness.

Then there was the night in Norfolk, two days before departure, on leave with Willie Bills and Tommy Bob and the rest, spoiling for fights with those from other services and states, drinking beer after beer, when they had cut through the park and he ducked down the embankment and into the bushes below. The relief was so great as he emptied himself, he at first did not even notice the other man beside him, uniformed too, holding himself as Morris did, but erect, his face tense with excitement. Morris knew now, admitted the hesitation, the instant skipped between realization and flight, in which fascination held him rooted, before he pushed the other soldier away and ran back up the slope.

"Lordy, Morris!" Tommy Bob bellowed. "See a ghost!"

But he offered no explanations.

The memories thumped out resounding and inevitable as oranges from a weak-cornered crate. By the time Jean Baptiste arrived — it had only been minutes really — Morris could respond to his greeting only with a look of resigned despair.

The Frenchman, overalled, a drawstrung cloth bag slung over his shoulder, cocked his head, concerned. "You are not well?"

Morris took a deep breath. "I'm all right. My head still hurts. The wine." He smiled wanly. "What's in the bag?"

"More wine," Jean Baptiste said, "bread, sausage, cheese, apples."

Morris laughed meanly. The anger of the early morning crept through him again. And contempt. "Do you want to eat here?"

"No. A place not far from here. It is very pretty."

Following Jean Baptiste through the woods, he was silent, a knot in his gut. He could feel his mouth twist: wine, a secret hiding place, probably a checkered tablecloth. It was grotesque, parodistic, and at various moments he intended to turn back. He watched Jean Baptiste, half lame, and felt his own leg aching with effort and the heat. Two cripples, he thought, and then ground the word into himself, like a cigarette into the skin: cripples, cripples. It filled him with calamitous delight.

It was a beautiful spot: the earth rolling up tree-dotted and green from a shallow brook; an abandoned outbuilding nearby; on the other bank the ruins of a farmhouse, its roof collapsed in perfect and ridiculous symmetry.

Morris settled into the thick grass. There was no table-cloth at least, only a couple of coarse napkins. Jean Baptiste set the meal, moving with a certain, antic grace. Morris half-listened to the Frenchman's endless monologue about trains, Marseilles, the War, imagined America, answering occasional questions in surly monosyllables, wondering why he stayed, willing himself to stand and stalk back to the château, and yet remaining, sullen, breaking bread, sharing the wine from the bottle, accepting the perfectly sliced eighths of apples, the cigarette Jean Baptiste offered and lit. He caught the Frenchman's glances, sometimes curious or wounded, but sometimes, too, disturbing: aware, calculating.

Inside, Morris felt his fury coiling, loathing gathering upon itself in tight rounds, waiting, weaving back and forth, judging the words, the moment. It grew tighter and tighter, straining desirous of release. Jean Baptiste was cautious — unnerved, Morris thought with sour pleasure — his patter continuing without joy. Obsessive.

Finally, there was silence. It lasted what seemed a very long time. Jean Baptiste's hand moved timidly over the grass upon which they lay and touched Morris's thigh.

"Whistle?" he said softly.

Morris shot to his feet, towering briefly over the French-man before Jean Baptiste sprang up, only for an instant slowed by his bad leg.

"*Je ne suis pas putain!*" Morris spat.

He was proud of those words painstakingly constructed as they ate, sprawled smoking, delivered with a sneer there in the face of that engineer dock rat.

He only heard it. A rustle. Moving air. He did not see it: Jean Baptiste's hand, the back of it, bones and knuckles sharp across his cheek and jaw. He stumbled; fell on his bad arm, yelping, his head adrift and skin aflame. Jean Baptiste spat into the grass.

Morris lay on the ground, his arm aching, the inside of his cheek bloodied against his teeth. But there was a deeper hurt. All the ire Jean Baptiste had engendered suddenly turned inward; Morris, like the stroked scorpion that stings itself and then, maddened, stabs its back again and again until death. The Frenchman gathered the food, corked the bottle and thrust it in the sack, all his movements unnaturally rapid, anger consuming itself in activity.

Morris watched dazed, but as the ankle shot by, his hand leapt to catch it, and at that instant of contact, he felt the jolt, like in the shell hole, as in the moment before the end in that last flickering of hope, and the sob exploded out of him helpless as a child's.

Jean Baptiste froze; remained suspended; sank slowly to earth.

"*Non. Non,*" he said. "*Non.*"

For a second or two, his fingers floated above the skin, before they buried themselves in Morris's hair.

"*Non. Maurice. Mon soldat, Maurice.*"

The soothing words, that name both his and not, fogged his mind, and the release that had lurched out in his first, hoarse cry now poured from Morris, infinitely sad, some lovely and terrible farewell to all that may be assumed in living.

There was no measuring of time then, there in that dappled place beneath the trees where the pain slowly dissolved, where again Morris felt that odd, stubbled face against his own and their hands wandered freely. Two cripples, Morris thought, smiling, full of a passion untried. There was a smell — musty, acrid — and he thrust himself toward sweat, toward the forbidden places that are closest to the animal in us: armpits and clefts and the backs of the knees.

Morris felt Jean Baptiste's fingers on the buttons of his tunic; pulling up his shirt. Again there were those whiskers unanticipated; then the tongue over his breasts; the tense flesh of his shoulders sucked into angry knots, then released in anemones of desire. He felt the chin shimmer through the line between his pectorals newborn of drills, of the calisthenics an ocean away. In him there was now no wish but abandon.

His fear surfaced suddenly as a diver.

"No. No." He squirmed away.

Jean Baptiste looked at him; held out his hand.

Morris smiled. "Okay. Okay. But not outside. There." He motioned toward the abandoned shed. "In there."

They staggered up together, slammed back the rusted hinges with their combined weight, then closed the door behind them so the only light was that which filtered through the spaces where shingles had tumbled down to meld with the straw below. Abashed as boys the first day of school, they took off their clothes, revealing bodies — which ought to have been unmarred — battered, wounded. Morris saw the scar than ran in a furious welt all down the leg of Jean Baptiste, the inept suturing of the moment emblazoned on his skin; his shoulder pocked too as if by buckshot. And Morris's souvenirs of manhood: the rosy keloid on his thigh; his arm torn in half a dozen places from lead and surgery.

They beheld each other in their imperfect nakedness. Then, without pretense or shame, they were enveloped wordlessly, each by the other, in perfect and passionate want.

In that afternoon that proceeded at once instant and stately, with some peculiar suspension or conflation of hours, Morris's eyes swept in sudden consciousness the straw, the walls, the golden rents in the overarcing gray of ceiling and beams, before their loss again to the rusty dark of his eyelids closed ecstatically or to the sleek and secret musculature of the French engineer. He felt some marvelful expansion, some unutterable doubling that plumbed his deepest self, as if here he had found his dark twin, that Morris unknown who had now escaped and might never be put back. He buried his face in the rough mustiness of that other body and breathed in himself, some forbidden, forgotten, desperate desiring of his whole life, and of that one moment he had confronted imminent destruction when there can be nothing but raw and final love.

And when it was done, when the gray above now was broken by the oblique rose of sunset, as they lay bare and exhausted on the itching straw, he felt the stubby hand of the engineer on his back, on the middle of his back, the cleft of his spine, and the voice drifted dreamlike to his ears:

"*Mon ami,*" it said.

"*Mon amour,*" it said.

"*Mon frère.*"

Fairy.

The word unspoken pulled your lips into a tight line of contempt as you watched him, watching you. He did not powder his face, slick his hair, but you saw it in his eyes. Your skin crawled as you neared him, over the lawn to the garden by the alley.

You curled your mouth upward on one side — enigmatic, perhaps seductive. You would not betray yourself. Morris Farrell was useful to you — might be, anyway — and there was no need to fear him. He would make no move, shell-shocked trackwalker with no future and an addled past. You would have no trouble getting what you needed from him.

"Good evening, Mr. Farrell." Head angled, hips thrown slightly to one side, at ease: the David.

"Evening, Mr. Skikey."

Oh, yes. You had seen them on Clark Street, in Tower Town, not just the perfumed boys with womanish faces, but the family men from Englewood, the Gold Coast, Evanston and Gary; learned to recognize that look of evaluation, that searching in Morris Farrell's eyes.

"Lovely time of year."

"Yes. Yes, indeed. Come July, though, we'll be wishing for the fall."

How you hated him: his simpleminded, small-town bearing, that broken-toothed half grin, his ultimate softness despite that growing bearishness of body. He had a fairy's foolish innocence, that pathetic desire to trust, to see his own feeble self in others. That you could exploit without the slightest qualm of conscience.

Pansies liked you, mistaking your polish and elegant dress for their own foppishness. In speakeasies, their eyes sought you out, beseeching when they were bounced out the door, as if they had counted on you for help. You had had to deal too with the men who, making the same error in judgment, taunted you. At first, you bore it; later, you were powerful enough to extract vengeance. At the very moment of insult, you shattered the kneecap of one of Aiello's runners with a single shot, to Capone's mixed surprise and delight. Certain others had fallen prey to you at the Four Deuces, in the cellar, after you had become its chiefest denizen.

"So, it's only three trains north and south each day?"

"Well, good trains. There's the mail run through about ten in the morning and two in the afternoon the other way, and the mixed train on the Connors branch three times a week."

"Lots of freight traffic though?"

"Oh, sure. A good deal of that."

"There seems to be. It must be every hour on the hour you can hear something going through."

"Not quite as regular as that. In the morning, the first one's the six-thirty-six, then the eight-nineteen . . ."

It strained you to stand there; made your back ache at the base of the spine where you concentrated all the tension so your face might be serene. You encouraged him, as you encouraged others: Justus Bechner, Maury Melrose, Sammy Pearlman at Western Union, another weakling — full of dreams and affected toughness, desperate for a guiding hand, someone to emulate, to befriend.

"I suppose I ought to wash up now, Morris."

He brightened at his name, as his sister had two days before when you, for the first time, called her Edna.

"Sure. Sure, Jay. I'll be along soon."

Slipping in the back door, you made a point to say, "What heavenly smells, Edna," as you passed the kitchen, though you did not pause to see if she were there. There would be no time to talk. In the mornings you cultivated her, while her brother slept and Justus Bechner slaved for the county. She provided a different sort of information than the men. And she warmed, of course, to any show of sympathy. Your contempt for her was different, perhaps even more profound. Her spinster homeliness affronted you; her dreary laboring seemed a charge laid on the world itself, a vengeance on life unearned. You knew ultimately what you wanted from her. The details were still imperfect, the timing unsure, but as you scrubbed your face before the bathroom mirror, the prospect brought a real smile to your lips, and you laughed softly.

After supper, you went for a walk, encountering Sammy as you knew you would in the easy twilight of the waning spring. He waved at you as you sauntered up the street, loitering as usual in front of his cobbler father's shop. As you approached, he bounced out of his accustomed squat and came to meet you, all gawkish eagerness.

"Hiya, Jay." He grabbed your hand and pumped it, proud at sixteen to call you by your first name. "Howya been?"

"Fine. Fine, thank you, Sammy. And you?"

"Pretty good. Pretty good. You have a chance to look over that magazine deal?"

"Oh, yes. Yes, that's the reason I came down this way. Would you like to walk awhile? You can tell me more about it."

You had not thought of the distribution scheme Sammy Pearlman had outlined two evenings before, nor so much as glanced at the smudged and folded sheets he had pressed upon you then. It made no difference. You needed only grunt as he chattered, assent to Sammy Pearlman's shrewdness, his dreams of a business that would provide him other opportunities, allow him to leave Christina behind. Even if, in a week or a month, you had to part with a few dollars, function — as Sammy put it — as his "capital source," it would be worth it to remain in favor with the boy who worked for Western Union.

"I don't know how you do it, Sammy," you said. "I suppose they've kept you even busier than usual down at the depot."

"Oh, brother! You know it. That son of a bitch Kiefer never lets up. He's jealous, I can tell you. He knows he'll still be running that damned office when I'm long gone. You know, he . . ."

He went on: unpredictable duties; small pay and smaller tips — a lackey's usual complaints. But you found out in passing that Mrs. Pike's sister had pneumonia; that the hardware store had sent an order for seeds they had somehow overlooked. With phones expensive and unreliable, Christina still conducted much of its business by wire. You were also informed that Callen McAlpern did not like you.

"You should have heard him with Kiefer. He thinks you're a faker. That's what he said. And Kiefer sat there like a stooge."

Sammy talked like a bad movie, or like the bad novels he read when he was not deep in some self-help manual. But you smiled, generously, and said: "No, I'm afraid Mr. McAlpern and I didn't hit it off too well. He's not a bad sort — "

"Don't kid yourself, Jay." Sammy Pearlman put his hand on your shoulder. "He's a crazy old bastard who can't stand the idea there's somebody else around here who's got more book smarts than he does. What's worse, he knows you've got instincts. I mean, I respect book smarts, but a man's got to have instincts like you and me, and Callan McAlpern never had a one of them."

He made you uncomfortable, deeply so. It was not his presumption or his silly plans, his whining, even his being a Jew. In him, you recognized another boy anxious for a mentor, a patron, a father or big brother. And you knew what that had cost him.

You had adjusted easily to life in the junkyard. Phelan seemed agreeable to your presence, to the addition of two more hands — tender and weak though they might be — and even more so to some companionship besides that of Wanda, the mutt bitch who on all but the coldest nights patrolled the yard, and who, according to Phelan, would have taken you to pieces mercifully faster but no less effectively than the rats had she discovered you in the drafty remains of that Chevrolet. Your mattress on the floor quickly came to seem home, one luxurious after bridge abutments and boxcars, and you worked conscientiously at learning the value of the castoffs that arrived daily, to judge furniture's condition, the salvageability of machinery, the quality of rags, sorting what might be redeemed from what should be consigned to the ash heap smoking in the far corner of the yard — all of this, knowledge you would never have dreamed existed in the lonely and autumnal world of your childhood. You rejected your former timid and bookish self — the shy boy solitary in his bastardy, lost in fantasies of places far away where French was spoken and days passed in effete pleasures — adopting instead the brute maleness of Phelan's world: heavy and noisy, full of stink and filth, coarse prejudices and curses you only half-comprehended. You hung on Phelan's every whispered word, his stories, the songs he croaked when he wheeled back from those whiskey-fueled adventures late at night, slamming doors, drawers, his own weight into everything around him, while you feigned sleep, thrilled and scared. That rasp, that souvenir of violence, amplified itself within you till it rattled your ears, a growl of true manhood you admired and wished your own.

Phelan was flattered. His towering, wide-girdled Irishness rocked with laughter when you damned the Italians or set yourself, purposeful if ineffective, to moving loads that would test even his strength. In the evenings, over soups and stews thick with beans and meat, washed down with bootleg beer, Phelan would tell you about O'Banion and Hymie Weiss, the North Side gangsters he served and respected even more than he hated the Wops of Johnny Torrio. "Chevy," Phelan called you for where he found you, rechristened for a machine engined and chromed, fast and potentially deadly. Chevy you might have happily remained all your life, or so you thought at the time.

"Now, look, Jay. It's still got some bugs, I know. I know that, Jay. But with a little cash, just a little financial . . ."

You nodded automatically, smiling, effortless and insincere. "Now, I told you. You worry about the details. Plan every step. When it's absolutely clear in your head, we'll take care of the investment. Even in a depression, Sammy, a man with instincts knows a good thing."

The look of dumb gratitude on his face, had you been someone other than you were, might have sparked in your heart some vague compassion, even affection. But you were too different to allow for such softness. After the good-byes, you watched Sammy Pearlman vanish into the gathering night, thankful for his stupidity and his conceit. Though he did not know it, you were doing him a favor. Out of this he would learn a hard lesson young. And cheaply.

You were asleep, warm and dreamless, almost a month into your new life of beer, oil, dirt, and sweat, of bootleggers' hidden trucks, of piles of the rejects of other people's lives. After dinner that night, you had drunk a second beer, then a third, as Phelan droned in his monotonous whisper about garbage and shotguns and girls. You were still not accustomed to drink. Most of what he said you barely heard, only words here and there as the alcohol made your senses sweet and soft. At some point, you had dozed off, waking in a start to find Phelan gone. He had asked you something just before you laid your head on the table, and laughed at your response. As you crawled onto your mattress, you tried to remember what it was the two of you had talked about. Outside, Wanda was barking at some passerby, or perhaps at some other boy destined for rat bait in the depths of the junkyard. But in that moment, you had been too deep in beery warmth to worry.

"Wake up! Come on! Wake up!"

The command filtered through layers of bubbles and weariness, an insistent murmur — "Wake up!" — soft, though the hand pawing and probing your shoulder was ungentle, demanding. It's Phelan, some voice of lounging consciousness told you, only Phelan.

"Wake up!"

Light pulled at your eyelids. Was it daytime? Time for work among the trash like St. Peter separating the saved from the damned: for the former the purgatory of the yard or the celestial realms of the upper floor, and for the rest, the fire smoldering eternally in back.

You stirred, lazily, unprepared for morning, your body unwieldy with sleep and beer. You moaned and screwed tight your eyes.

"Wake up!"

And it was wrong: the light electric, and in Phelan's whisper a slur that told you he was not sober. You knew it was still night, and through lingering dreaminess wondered why he waked you.

"Oh, Phelan. Let him alone. He's a kid, for God's sake!"

There was a laugh, a drunken bray that resolved itself in a soprano giggle. You shot upright, your eyes bugging and squinting as Phelan's face took shape before you, beyond it another form.

"What?"

"Wake up, Chevy, you little son of a bitch."

"Oh, he's a sweet one, ain't he?" The giggle again. "They don't make them that pretty in this part of town."

"Better watch it, Sally. He might show you a thing or two." Phelan laughed, that wheezing between a hiss and a rattle.

The figure behind Phelan came into focus: a woman, a large, round woman, Polish probably, blond with short-cropped hair, a tight dress, weaving slightly back and forth, though in that instant you could not tell whether it was she who moved, or you. Your head ached.

"I told you it was a good deal, Sally. Wouldn't sell you

wrong. You awake, Chevy?" He slapped your shoulder. "Get ready, boy. We don't have all goddamn night!"

You breathed deep, trying to clear your mind, to understand what Phelan said. But the fog within broke only sparsely. Too, there somewhere far inside, there was some petty irritant, some speck like a mote in the eye that would not let you concentrate.

"Hell, Sally. You do it. You get him up." Phelan laughed again. "Yeah, you get him up."

You uncoiled in a stretch, trying to cast off the sleep that pressed upon you. Vaguely, you remembered Phelan's voice from when your head had slipped toward the table after dinner: "Time you learnt then, Chevy. We'll take care of it good. Time you learnt."

A hand stroked your back; kneaded your neck. Smooth fingers furrowed your hair where your skull swelled. Warm breath tickled your ear, and your chin rose slightly as that hand moved to smooth your beardless cheek.

"Oh, you teach him good, Sally. You teach him."

You heard the giggle again, as a second hand now slipped beneath the oversized shirt of Phelan's you wore at night: whispered across your ribs toward your heart.

Deep within you — beyond thought, beyond memory — that speck, transformed now to a ball, began to quicken. It pulsed slowly at first, alternately hot and cold. No, it said. No.

The fingers moved over you still, across your chest to your throat, under your jaw. You rocked softly, silently, recollecting Phelan's question: "You never did it?" And your voice, thick and foolish: "Nope." And Phelan: "Time you learnt."

Now it was a steady beat inside you, ice of fear, heat of

rage: No. No. A darkness rolled over you, carrying the whisper of another name, another place. The hands on your back chilled you, worse than the worst winds of the worst nights you roamed the streets.

"You get him going, Sally. Like you get me going. You'll get it tonight, girl. We'll bang your bells!"

No.

The word gathered strength at that hidden point within you; your body stiffer and stiffer as it throbbed along your nerves.

"Keep your pants up, you old bull. Give me time!" Her touch sharp as sleet across your shoulders. "Now, come on, honey. You're like a board. Sally'll be good to you. She knows what to do."

She pulled you to her suddenly, violently, your face buried in the breasts exposed by her unbuttoned blouse. Her hand slithered now through the first hairs of your groin.

"Come to Momma."

All throughout you was a terrible shuddering, every muscle and bone torquing so it seemed you would fly into pieces brittle as glass.

No.

"Fuck her. Fuck her!" The voice whistled hoarse like the wind off the Lake. "Fuck her. Put it in. Put it in!"

"Come on, honey. Relax. Be a good boy. Come to Momma. Come."

Then it ruptured, that tiny, throbbing ball, shooting its energy through you. You turned hard as steel, cold as brass as her fingers grasped the limpness of you shrinking into yourself. This would not happen. Phelan was here. Phelan would not let this happen.

"No!"

The word rocketed to the ceiling, shattered there in a million shards of negation like a holiday skyrocket as your rigid body exploded in a star burst of kicks and punches. "No! No!" like ancillary missiles blew out of you as Sally reeled back squealing. "No!"

"You bastard! You bastard!"

You did not care. This was what you were.

"You bastard! Phelan! You bastard!"

You crumpled, exhausted, barely hearing for the blood pounding in your ears.

"Bring me here to fuck a goddamn fairy! You fuck him! I'll get you for this, Phelan! Think you can get me cheap for some fairy!"

"Sally! Sally!"

"Get your goddamn dick in your pants. You think I'm gonna spread my legs for you in front of this yodeler! I'll get you, Phelan. This'll be all over goddamn Chicago tomorrow, you queer. Dion O'Banion'll run your ass out of here. You can go down with the stinkin' Wops where you belong, and your little cocksucker, too!"

You were still sitting on the mattress, rocking again, listening, watching as if from a great distance. Sally swirled back into her clothes, shrieking, as Phelan, drunk and dumbfounded with his fly unbuttoned, stood speechless. As Sally's anger billowed, all that seemed to change in Phelan was the scar across his throat, blanching from that milky pink to a white beyond snow or goose down or babies, some utterly unnatural absence of color that might be found in the heat of the center of the sun. The woman dervished by him in a whirl of insults, slamming the door with a thunderclap that shook you even in your stupor.

Then there were the two of you. You filled with the power of denial, though even then you vaguely realized it had stunned and perhaps even hurt this Sally with whom you had no quarrel. But still, you felt as if a cloud over you had dissipated. You looked toward Phelan, stupid with thanks for you were not sure what.

You had no time to consider it, understand it, voice it. Nor to fear. He crossed the room in three steps. Had he closed his fist, the blow would have broken your jaw, perhaps snapped your neck, for your head smashed so hard against the wall from only the flat of his hand you were, for an instant, close to senseless, your vision pinpointing toward nothingness, your ears staticked by a ringing that would linger for days. Pain seared half your face, and the taste and smell of blood choked you, surging from your mouth and nose.

He struck you again, wild-eyed with whiskey and rage. His next blow caught you in the stomach, lifted you from beneath the covers that remained to you, sent the burn of galled beer into the back of your throat and somewhere just below your eyes.

You understood suddenly you might die there on that mattress. You began to struggle as his hand this time slammed flat against your temple and sent you sprawling over the floorboards, his rasping voice penetrating imperfectly that consciousness splintered by a thousand detonations of pain and perplexity and terror: "Yodeler! Goddamn lose me my piece of ass! Got her for you! You like that? Goddamn your ass! Like it! You'll . . ."

You — for beer, for sleep invaded, for shock, for the past, for the beating, for fear of death — had no strength left.

You were hardly aware now where you were or what had happened. The blows stopped. You ached. You bled. Fingers sought the hair at the back of your head, the nape of your neck, sought it and twisted it.

"You goddamn fairy! You want it! You take it! Now! You take it now!"

The whole weight of Phelan fell upon you, over your back and legs, thrusting furiously. And you, like a man cast into the pit, like the soul whose final shriek is all his hope blown to chaos, began to scream. You screamed as he grunted over you. You screamed and screamed, your only reply the howling of the mutt bitch in the yard outside, singing like Cerberus at your betrayal.

V

NEXT DAY— the very next morning after we all had supper there with Edna and Morris — Callan's off to the Sheriff to ding him good about finding out about Jay. Now Callan, over the years, he'd made a regular habit of dinging the Sheriff about one thing or another. It's like it's in the blood. But the Sheriff — Paul Beckner (no relation, spelt with a k) — well, he didn't take to the idea. There's no love lost there.

But you can't put old Callan off. Like I said, he's one terrier of a man. Those first couple days, Beckner told him he had enough troubles without checking up on some tourist who hadn't done harm to anybody, and even if it was true he wasn't using his real name that there was no law against that (mind, now, I'm telling you what he said), that a man could call himself Mary Five-Fingers if he took it into his head and, long as he didn't cheat anybody or rob him or something like that, it was nobody's business, including the Sheriff's.

No is a word Callan never quite learned. I'd see him every morning at the courthouse on his way upstairs, up to see Paul, and it turns out finally Beckner couldn't put up with all the bothering and promised Callan he'd look into things, which he did do, though he took his own sweet time about it, which meant probably that Jay was with us longer than he might've been.

I could never quite ponder out why he did stay around. Jay Skikey was nobody's fool, and he must've pegged Callan as trouble as soon or sooner than Callan pegged him. Here he is, on the lam like they say, skipping out on some real nasty business up in Chicago, looking for a place where nobody knows him, a place he can lie low for a spell, when — Bang! — along comes old Callan when he's barely here a couple weeks. You'd think he'd've figured it out and hightailed it out of here the next day.

He didn't though. Just stayed around and went through his days like he always did, jawing with Edna and me and Morris, talking to Maury down at the bank, getting to know a few other people, taking tea with Mrs. Pike, the piano teacher, like he's still testing the waters to settle down. Now it turns out he was doing some other checking here and there. On train schedules, for one thing. Not just the passenger trains, the freights too, hanging around the station and probably milking old Morris for all he was worth. With the Western Union boys, too. Nothing suspicious. He was one smooth son of a gun, old Jay. He sent out a few wires and got to know the folks around the office, especially the delivery boys, because, you know, they're always snooping where they shouldn't be and they'll blab anything they've heard, smelt, or seen if somebody treats them nice. That

Pearlman boy, especially. Him and Jay were thick as thieves. Looks to me like he knew his days here were numbered, but he wasn't going to clear out any sooner than he had to.

Now why, I can't say. Maybe he thought nobody'd pay Callan any mind, or that somehow he'd win him over. Maybe he was a cocky so-and-so who had it we were such a bunch of country boys we'd never outsmart him. Maybe he liked the danger. I mean, it must be pretty exciting being a gangster, and sitting around a place like Christina must've seemed pretty tame for somebody like that. So, Callan gave him a bit of worry that he kind of liked.

But I think — I know this sounds funny — I like to think that it was Edna. Lots of people, right after she ran off, figured she was in cahoots with him, that the two of them had planned things out before, that she knew who he was all along. I could never quite buy into that. I don't deny he had a power over her. Lord sakes, anybody could see that. She jumped me good about Callan, about the way he acted at supper, like it was my fault! The way she hung on everything Jay said, it got a little embarrassing.

Still, well . . . I'd never seen her bloom like that. It was . . . sweet, I guess. Gave me a funny, good feeling. Supper'd be late because she'd gone in to change her clothes. Edna Farrell! I tell you, she got to looking almost pretty while Jay was here, as pretty as she could look. She started taking care like she never had before. I like to think he noticed, that maybe that gangster had a spot in his heart for her, too, and that he gave the old girl a little, you know, affection.

That wasn't the only talk, though — the talk about Jay and Edna. There was even some rumors about Jay and, well,

Morris. Now, Morris Farrell was one queer fellow, but he wasn't queer that way, if you know what I mean. I'd stake my life on that and my Buick along with it. I lived around the man for years, and I can guarantee you I don't think any thought of s-e-x ever crossed his mind, much less anything unnatural. I know I'm a small-town boy, and since I was too young, I wasn't in the War and didn't see the kind of sin that goes on over there in Paris and places like that, like maybe Morris did. But working for the county, I've had occasion to go to the capital, and I've been to meetings in Kansas City and down in New Orleans, and I saw some things I'd have to be drunk to mention even in impolite company. I'm nobody's babe in the woods.

When that kind of talk started after Morris was killed . . . Well, the one time somebody brought it up to my face — now it was a friend of mine and he wasn't saying it himself exactly, just letting me know that this kind of thing was getting said — he brought it up and I took him by the lapel (not hard, you understand, but to make sure he could tell I was serious), and I said to him: "Look here. I think I knew Morris Farrell as well or better than anybody else in Christina, and I'd never say Morris wasn't about the oddest duck I've ever come across, but he was as good and Christian a man as this town ever saw, and you can tell so-and-so if he wants to go gossiping like some old biddy" — that's not the word I used — "about the dead, well, he better not be doing it around me if he knows what's good for him."

That's the last I heard about it. I mean, Morris was a funny one, and Lord knows what went on in that head of his. But damn it, I say there's a certain kind of talk you just can't allow.

◆ ◆ ◆

At night, he would think of Jay Skikey.

There in the dark, the picture formed: the two of them at the back of the property, him with the watering can, Jay next to him, talking softly, talking about not much of anything. Asking about Christina, Edna, family in general, about Morris, taking an interest in walking track, in how many trains came through mornings, noons and nights. Morris humored him, mustered the energy to speak in complete sentences and even tell a sort of joke now and then, though he was so long out of practice that he'd find himself winding down the switchback almost exhausted from the effort.

But he would think less about what was said than about Jay Skikey himself. He was younger than Morris, somewhere in his undefinable twenties, though he had a kind of confidence and ease that sometimes made him seem much older. His body was one not so long blossomed into manhood; his bearing that of someone proud of his looks, who knew that heads turned when he walked by, that he shone like a starling among sparrows, mysterious as Valentino. He claimed to be an orphan, and was vague as to how he had acquired all that polish and tremendous self-possession at so young an age. Morris rather liked that, on occasion inventing scenarios on his walks to the Junction and back about Jay Skikey's past as a small-town waif; product of some laundry-festooned ghetto in the vast, industrial North; an optimistic child immigrant fleeing the European conflagration barely after his voice had changed; the disinherited scion of some mercantile czar of New York or Chicago.

And Morris would imagine him naked, indulging himself in that pantry turned bedroom where, for so many years, he had fought to banish any image of desire. It was not merely the coloring — the blackness of the hair, the dark skin and astonishing eyes — but the type of body — not stocky but solid, thickening in an admirable way — that recalled Jean Baptiste. Morris allowed his imagination of more than thirty to undress Jay Skikey in the garden, in the dining room, in the privacy of his 4:00 A.M. bed as it willed, delighting in every curve and angle — shoulder, belly, bottom, and crotch — extrapolating the Professor of Aesthetics's own excitement.

It had been that way in France.

In France, after they were dressed again, and they had walked back to the clearing, when Jean Baptiste was gone and Morris had climbed the path, steps, and stairs in the gathering dark; after the lights were extinguished and those others — Micheletti, Lansdowne — snored in the tranquil ward, Morris had lain awake in vertiginous horror and elation, with the palpable result of a swelling beneath his nightshirt, one that shamed him though it was utterly disguised by counterpane and darkness; one that, in the midst of all those drugged, exhausted, pain-distracted slumbers, he could relieve without the slightest fear. Even if the sheets were stained, Millie would be too discreet to mention anything, and the worst he might expect was an oblique comment from the surgeon that his recovery was obviously accelerating. Then again, they would probably all assume that any shedding of seed was the involuntary sign of dreams, the inevitable product of an invalid's frustration.

Thus, even that first night, after an entire afternoon of

play, he indulged himself alone, so he could sleep, but even more so he could remember the electricity he had known in those hours — he thought smiling — those hours in the hay. He masturbated quietly, purposefully, fully expecting at the end of it a nauseated fury, the kind that had flickered through him after each release that afternoon, that Jean Baptiste had somehow been prepared for, had battled and vanquished again and again as they explored yet another avenue of play. But when he was done, when his teeth ground tight to deny voice to the slightest moan, he found himself disturbed and elated that all that washed through him was a sweet relaxation. The snores, the occasional groan, even the shuffling of the night nurse through the ward all became soothing as the sound of lapping water, drawing him gently, satisfied, toward sleep.

In the morning, the fear returned. It was then Christina was strongest. When the doctor made his rounds, when Millie watched him exercise, Morris felt shaky, accelerated, as if, merely by looking at him, they might know what had happened and draw back to denounce him to the entire ward, the Army, America, Christina. Yet neither Millie nor the doctor, Micheletti, Lansdowne, nor anyone else took much notice of his agitation, or they explained it easily away.

"Calm down," Millie said. "You're trying too hard."

He realized then that only he might betray himself. His previous day's pleasure was his own; had some obscure place in the order of things so no leprosy had disfigured his face or letter emblazoned itself on his bosom. He went to town that afternoon with a peculiar lightness in his step, met Jean Baptiste with the casual intimacy of an old friend, drank wine, and made arrangements for the following day. On the way home, he was amazed at his easy violation of what in Christina, in Norfolk, in the trenches, even two days before, would have struck him as monstrous.

In those three weeks (he would remind himself there alone with his fantastical Jay Skikey that, in France, it had been but three weeks), he and Jean Baptiste from Perpignan played out what real passion Morris was to know in his whole life. In that outbuilding, in the woods, swimming where the brook widened into a small pond with a bed of rushes, in Jean Baptiste's room hard by the tracks, even once in the newborn night in the clearing below the château, barely undressed, they loosed Morris's respectable moorings, the same ones Jean Baptiste had untied as a near child in Marseilles, Morris hoping somehow his neophyte enthusiasm made up for his friend's wiser experience. He felt himself some wild combination of La Salle, Coronado, Balboa — exploring rivers, canyons, caverns unknown — and simultaneously, like America itself, some vast territory to be traversed, surveyed, spelunked, subdued. All senses were renewed, refined: smell, taste, pain that dissolved into delight, nerves never before touched that bloomed in electric flowerings of wanting ever more intense. And for all this, he knew — there afterward in the hospital bed he held now tenuously, only for a few weeks more, perhaps a couple months — he owed a certain debt to Carmichael, who had unwittingly showed Morris his true self in that instant before the possibility of awful death that makes any desire expressing life and love not only forgivable but necessary. But it was to Jean Baptiste that he owed the knowledge that such gestures might come not only in moments when the danger of ultimate loss looms beyond the questionable safety of the crater's lip.

All this returned to him sweetly on his descent from, ascent to Christina, the ties familiar beneath his feet; in the solitude of his early morning bed. For the first time since Ste. Claire, Morris felt some connection to the wider world; without fear of disaster, he was sharing with someone, still only words outright, innocuous ones over the spatter of a watering can. In all those years, it was not personal exposure, not hysterical or sniggering accusation that had drawn him so deep within himself, but something far worse — that fatality of his desirings he confronted in Varennes Ste. Claire one unforgettable afternoon. After that moment, he no longer noticed Millie, the doctor, his own increasing strength. They might have sent him back to combat finally, right before the Armistice, if the decision were simply one of physical wholeness. He had healed admirably. In the end, the doctor's therapy had brought his body back almost as potent as it had been before Belleau Wood.

But they would never allow him to return to the front. He could tell by their expressions, by his own sudden and, for them, inexplicable tears, by his silence, by the look of vague but certain and utter loss that possessed his face as he stared at the ceiling of the ward, at those nursery pentimentos on the walls, willing all his attention toward that blankness, toward those figures that might be captured only indistinctly, so as to drive away the nightmares of his own experience and his ineffable intuition that he was the cause of catastrophe, that the realization of his wanting led inevitably to the destruction of whatever he chose to desire.

Now, with the lapse of fifteen years, he felt freed by this elegant and beautiful Professor of Aesthetics. Even Edna — poor Edna, whom he loved with a mix of blood and pity — seemed to recognize Jay Skikey's specialness. And Skikey, broad-hearted, treated her kindly, better perhaps than any boarder had ever done, even than Justus, who to Morris seemed still less a member of the family than a piece of furniture — a buffet, armoire, one of those large, functional pieces in a room inevitably assigned to a wall — and even he responded to Jay. Jay Skikey was, for Morris, the avenue for his return to the world.

There was no War. Morris knew no War would snuff Jay Skikey out, and if he stayed or didn't, he would nonetheless allow Morris's recapture of what had been buried since an oppressive summer day in a small French town, when he concluded his kiss was worse than that of Judas: one not of betrayal but of death.

◆　　◆　　◆

It was your refinement that betrayed you.

Sprawled on the bed of your rented room, it made you laugh. Better that Beak or Tonyo or Capone himself had fled here, gross as the salesmen these people were used to, the tourists with extra money to spend and canned Rotarian haleness. But not you. You should have ignored the advice in Chicago: "Not Hot Springs. They'll be on the lookout in Hot Springs. People from up here go to Hot Springs. Christina. There's a sleepy little burg! Who'd ever think to look there? You can hole up for months. Years!"

It had taken hardly three weeks for Christina to find you out.

The fault was yours. You had underestimated them, using that nickname you had cherished. You yourself came from such a town — an unimportant place, where an undertaker might enjoy a certain status, where a native son come home again would value his wider culture like a battle star. Callan

McAlpern or his equivalent — some teacher, preacher, mystically inclined crackpot — would need little time and less motivation to unmask you.

Sammy told you: "Beckner's sent out wires. Are you in some kind of jam? Kiefer was real secret about it, but I sneaked a look and saw your name. I mean, a friend's a friend, right?"

You had agreed, pleased those interminable chats about magazine subscriptions had finally borne fruit. The news itself did not surprise you. Since that dinner — Johnny Skikey, indeed! — you had expected it. Of course McAlpern would pester the law eventually. You knew the type: sly, vaguely queer, a perfect politician, by nature duplicitous and utterly determined. The Sheriff had no quarrel with you; might not even have registered your presence in this town accustomed to passers-through, though you, the first time you glimpsed him, etched his face, his build, and your impression of his character on your mind. He was a pacific man, one who dealt with trouble only as it arose, not seeking it out for his unconscious certainty of evil's dominion in this world. Beckner, like most of the few honest policemen you had known, had neither great ambitions nor crusader's zeal, unlike Callan McAlpern, who found Christina's canvas too small a one on which to paint his dreams, though for his own, doubtless perverse reasons sought out no other, and so insisted on exposing you when you intruded on his world.

You should have left. There on the bed in the dark, the house silent around you, you knew that. A man so astute saw it was merely a matter of time before the consequences of an undertaker's reading of the *Divine Comedy* exploded over you.

But you remained, though you had begun to take precautions. Each day's passage made escape less certain. At first, you preferred to see your delay as a response to boredom, a toying with chance that sent adrenaline through you as it had in your days as torpedo, machine gun in hand. Now, there in the darkness, you knew with the years your taste in such games had grown far more refined. It was such sophistication that kept you here.

It was the sister and brother, the lonely woman teetering always on hysteria; the catatonic man, a bundle of disasters ambulating back and forth over railroad ties, maimed as sure as if his throat were parted by a raging scar. You knew these people, and they waked within you obscure desires, unalloyed, that compelled you to stay, propelled you toward acts of a sublimity you had not yet experienced.

You lit a cigarette; wished you had a drink. Justus Bechner snored next door, and you envied briefly his loutishness, that truculent stupidity that gave his life, thoughts, motives a wonderful predictability, made them seem almost a kind of biological response. The world was full of microbes in the shape of men. They made up the gangs top to bottom in Chicago, the lot of them full finally of a mindless emotion that assured, one night, theirs would be the second finger on the trigger. They had such a paltry appreciation of wickedness, their lives directed toward petty tokens of transcendence: guns, cars, easy women, flashy jewels. All little Capones, they dreamt of rolls of twenties in their pockets, dispensed to bellboys and hatcheck girls who would contemplate such bills with awed delight. Despite the blood on their hands, hopelessly, foolishly, even those gangsters wanted to be loved.

It made you laugh. You, the man without history: first

abandoned, then betrayed. You: not simply denied love or full of hate, but subjected to a flame so fierce that, sure as some alchemical magic, it had transformed all love that might exist or have existed in you. Women and men you loathed equally, the young and the old, the healthy and sick. And in Chicago, for a time, at the behest of those who would truly never understand, you made a world where all your fury might speak.

The first time, it was Angelo. It was a test of your loyalty incidental to the matters that truly concerned them. Two of Capone's bodyguards found you, brought you to the cellar. Angelo was tied to a chair, and you smiled as you realized he had been fool enough to double-cross them. Angelo: your defender, the man who saved you from Rocco and guided you through that initiatory rite on the North Shore. Now he was blindfolded, helpless; doomed for making a few hundred dollars on the side. They wanted to know whom he had sold to, into whose hands he had diverted that whiskey, fifth by fifth, in the last six months. Penny-ante. Small time. You felt something like pity.

They beat him. It was stupid and brutal, there in the basement beneath the speakeasy, the gaming tables, the cribs on the top two floors. There in the bowels of Chicago. They cracked his jaw with blackjacks, broke his teeth. He refused to talk, soon would be unable to anyway, and then would either faint or die before he told them what they wanted to hear.

"Stop it!' you shouted.

You felt the man beside you draw away as if you had emitted a tubercular cough. The eyes falling on you glinted with suspicions confirmed, your words the proof of your own complicity. You met the glares coolly, strolling toward the man bound to the chair.

"What is it you need to know?"

They told you.

"Give me a half hour. Cigarettes, matches, a book of pins. A knife. Pliers."

Though later you would use other methods, those few things were all you ever needed. Those, and a captive incapacitated. Then, you could find out anything, make lies real, discover information as yet unthought of. You drew from your recollections of anatomy, of history, of art and the hagiography of saints, and by application of that knowledge, learned all you might have wished of the human soul and more. Some extreme unctionist bearing promises not of heaven but hell, you heard things man was never intended to hear, such confessions as St. Peter might expect in that last instant of explanation, exculpation.

You did not forgive. You took what was offered, demanded more, and killed. Till the last no one escaped you. All the others vanished finally down the tunnel and out the trapdoor on the alley, for the ride to the river, the sewer, the abandoned brickyards and rock quarries on the southern outskirts.

Till the last one. You shattered his balls. You had learned how in a history of the Templars. You had done it to Angelo and watched his screaming unmoved. He was the man who had saved you. Men had saved you before.

But you had small use for salvation. Only by death might a victim escape you, and so Fat Angelo died, and O'Donohue, and Kusulski, and Sweet Lucy Berrigan who had fingered Rossetti for Bugs Moran. Bonavena and Hop

Toad Guita's cousins and Rosy Morrell and all those others whom you remembered not by their names but by their sufferings. You broke every one, including the last. You had made him your creature. He could do nothing proud but die.

But they made you spare him, those lieutenants who now gave orders since Capone had boarded the train for the penitentiary in Atlanta. That night, as they hauled that still breathing lump of flesh away to dump on his home turf as an example, you knew the gang was rotten in Chicago, and your days as its Grand Inquisitor were numbered. You had wrenched from that Irishman all human possibility. He was only a ghost, but one who could still speak.

They set him free.

Within a week, the papers, the Chicago Crime Commission, and Bugs Moran all had your name.

Which had brought you in only a few weeks to this room in a boardinghouse in Christina. No longer yours, the dark kingdom in the cellar of 2222 Wabash Avenue; you yourself no longer Dandy Allan, The Doctor, The Professor, The Angel. No. J. Skikey, an itinerant man of refinement. That identity too would have to go, obliterated as so much else in your life had been. You needed now another avatar and a different venue. You had to create yourself anew so you might continue your career of pain.

First, though, there were final matters to be resolved in this godforsaken town by this Professor of Aesthetics, such matters as might please him, might satisfy his will. And with that happy prospect easy on your mind, you slept.

VI

I T WAS pretty much an accident, so the story goes, pretty much one of those funny right place, right time, right folks kind of things you hear about every now and then. Otherwise, hell, Jay might be living up on the mountain. With all of Callan's bellyaching, poor old Paul Beckner finally sends out a couple inquiries: description, "known as," "claims to be," "some reason for suspicion." Friends is what he sent them to, fellows he knew for one reason or another down toward Shreveport and up toward Mockdon County.

But imagine it — it's like some things are meant, that Providence has a hand somehow — one of the Rhymers Creek boys has a friend up in Kansas City, and for some reason, he lets this buddy up there know about Beckner's information, and that buddy in Kansas City, he's got a couple fellows he knows who, lo and behold, are G-men. He passes the story along — now this is only about two weeks after that dinner we all had with Callan — and that quick, the Federal boys are real interested in Christina and this stranger who wants to be its Professor of Aesthetics.

Now, before they sashay down here — they're not coming from Kansas City unless they've got good reason; all those G-men are just East Coast boys who can't find a damned address if the streets aren't named for numbers — they get some telegrams down to Beckner, and you know Jay found out about them, being thick with the kids at Western Union. They wouldn't even have to tell him directly what was in the wires. Letting him know Beckner was getting telegrams from Kansas City would've probably been enough. These days, they'd've caught him, since we got the phones straightened out. They'd've called from Kansas City. Back then was before we were hooked up real good, before they took the phones away from Mildred McNutt, who'd had them from the very beginning and listened in on everybody and could never be bothered with long distance. But Jay'd've probably figured out a way to take care of that, too. So there were telegrams back and forth and some special delivery letters, and from what Callan told us later, they got a pretty good picture from them of old Jay Skikey.

There's a hard man to figure. But I got the story from Callan and I got it from Paul Beckner, and they got it from the Federals so who am I to doubt it? It goes that Jay was an orphan. We knew that much from what he'd said, but we didn't know any details. A man's past is his own, I always say. Anyway, he didn't grow up in one of those homes. Some spinster aunt, I guess, she took him in when he was a baby. According to what Beckner heard, she was the one who brought him up. That's where all that culture came from.

In that town where he lived, I imagine, they probably thought he was pretty strange. I bet he was a lonely little fellow, there with an old lady who made him learn French and probably dressed him funny and didn't let him play much because she didn't want him mussed up. But he learned everything she wanted, seems like. Then, when he was sixteen, he walked out, just left that old lady alone without so much as a fiddle-de-dee and ended up in Chicago.

She died. Up and died. It wasn't six months, so the report said, that she gave up the ghost, poor single lady who'd given the best she had for Jay. I admit, it's probably not the best thing for a boy to be brought up by a maiden aunt, but still, he owed her something, don't you think? Makes it look like he must've been a pretty coldhearted fellow from the very start.

So, off he goes to Chicago, and you have to figure in those first few months it was hand to mouth. I've never been in Chicago, but we all know it's a fast town, and coming from some speck of a place, old Jay must've had to scramble. They don't really know how he did it. There wasn't much in the report about it — there wasn't much in the whole thing really — but he was probably learning some tough lessons. Before too long, though, somewhere along in the early twenties, he wiggled his way in with some of the right people. Well, the right people if you're in that line of work. It's around that time he starts getting a reputation as Dandy Allan. That wasn't his real name, of course, but he'd tossed that out easy as he'd walked away from that old lady. He had some other nicknames. The Professor was one I can remember, which makes sense. Anyway, he got in thick with some of the real big-timers up there, and I mean big ones, like Capone.

I don't like to speak ill of folks, and like I've said, far as I know and never mind all the gossip, which was just that, gossip, Jay Skikey was a gentleman through and through the whole time he was here in Christina. But, according to that report, according to what Paul said and Callan told me, he made his name up there not just because he could talk French and Italian and dressed like a prince. What got him in good with the gang was — you'll pardon me — that he was one mean son of a bitch. In the papers and the *Police Gazette* and places like that, we all read about what Capone and Legs Diamond did to people who crossed them. But from what the report said — now this is all secondhand and probably Callan'd've wanted to make old Jay look as black as the devil himself, but Paul Beckner didn't have reason to, and he tells pretty much the same story — well, Dandy Allan was famous for that kind of thing. He was the gang's man for the third degree.

Even Callan, when he talked about it, shied when it came to saying outright what the Federals put in that report, but Paul — him being law enforcement, I suppose he knows better or he's more used to the awful things people can do — he told me some about what Jay did, and I'd swear on a stack of Bibles, it was gruesome. Gives me a chill even now to think about it. Ugly, ugly things. Up there, they said Jay always got what he wanted out of you, or what the bosses wanted. I bet even they were scared of him, those Italians. Lord, he must've been hard. He must've had meanness stored up since he was a baby to do what they said he did. It can't've just been being an orphan. There's lots of people who lost family and even grew up in those homes who turn out fine, good men who get married and have kids and are a credit to the community. But Jay . . . After he was done, well, when he was done getting what he wanted . . . The word's mangled, I guess, like a cat does with a bird. He played with them to make them talk. The kind of thing you read about the Germans doing in the War, or like those priests in Spain way back when.

This is the fellow who's living next door to me, mind. Not the next house down, but right beside me on the same hallway and shaving in the same sink and soaking in the same bathtub. This is the fellow who's treating Edna better than any boarder except maybe me has ever treated her in her whole life and actually getting Morris — Morris Farrell — to chew the fat out there in the garden and even over the table. It doesn't make a whole lot of sense, does it?

Well, it turns out things started to get real hot for Jay up in Chicago. With the Crash, I guess everything started to go sour for the gangsters even, and then Prohibition's pretty much a lost cause, what with FDR promising to get rid of it, and Capone's in jail. The G-men have got a good lead on Jay, something it sounds like they really hadn't had before. Some stool pigeon's fingered him as the one who, ah, the one who'd made it so he doesn't have to worry, about, well, let's say, getting his girl in trouble, if you see what I mean. So, I guess he gets some cards printed up and hightails it out of Chicago down to Kansas City and picks up the *Bonnie Blue,* and all of a sudden he's boarding at the Farrells'.

Beckner says the Federals figured he was still hiding out in Chicago or had gone East, and I'll bet you those fellows in Kansas City thought they were headed for a promotion for sure on account of what they'd picked up by accident. It didn't work out quite that way, of course. Jay was one slippery character. When the time came, he vanished like a puff of smoke. Right when they thought they had him.

◆　◆　◆

There in the ripe spring, Morris found himself for the first time whistling on occasion as he stepped down through the sunset. It did not surprise him. Those ghosts — companions spiritual almost corporeal who had so long accompanied him on his journeys to and from Christina — were now memories, what they were supposed to be, a veteran's sad but long-past recollections. Jay Skikey, his unabashed desire for Jay Skikey, had freed him from the spell of Carmichael and Jean Baptiste, allowed him to recall them as he never had before, relive the lost pleasures and confront without terror or the assumption of blame what had become of them.

He did not know what would occur with the Professor of Aesthetics. He fantasized sometimes driving Justus Bechner from the house, moving upstairs, deceiving Edna — naive and true — once Jay's mutual desire were established. Morris had few doubts, for who, in all the years, had ever treated him as Jay did? Who had stood in that special way? From whose eyes had he known that look of evaluation but Jean Baptiste's?

Or perhaps they should go elsewhere. Leave Christina. Move west to California. A Professor of Aesthetics could establish himself anywhere, and surely in the valleys and mountains along the Pacific, there was a need for a man who walked track. Or perhaps he would find some other work, something more lucrative, less solitary, for Morris suddenly felt a rush of possibilities he had not felt in fourteen years, the sweet and secret blossoming of the whole world given him by that man who might have been Jay Skikey's brother, that man Morris Farrell had loved.

For the first time voluntarily, there at the curve before the entrance to the switchback where the ghost of Jean Baptiste was wont to join him, he recalled the end of it, what had convinced him of his own damnation. It had been only three weeks since that ludicrous picnic. In that time, they had been together a dozen times. At the château, the doctors remarked on his greater progress, his recovery accelerating day to day. He would grin mysteriously at what would be to them the appalling secret of his health. He found himself hopelessly intrigued with his own physicalness, that thing so nearly lost on the battlefield. In the dark, he would touch himself, not only sexually but simply to know his body, sense tactilely what his lover knew and compare it with what he had discovered of the engineer. Not to compete — to find a muscle larger here, skin more ductile there — but to capture nuance, the peculiar variations in bodies ostensibly related in the most profound ways which nonetheless differed subtly, while in a hundred manners more, they reflected, remade, duplicated each other.

He arrived at Varennes Ste. Claire that afternoon prepared for love. The plans had been laid for three o'clock: Jean Baptiste's room with white wine, which left Morris less drunk than red. He had bought apples — half green, palm size, tart — and ate one as he waited in front of the Quatre Chats, greeting the familiar faces, his arm no longer a-sling, in his last days in the town, he sensed, before they declared him cured and fit for service again. He drove that from his head as he waited, not knowing of the new heat of battle at the front, picking up such news only gradually from the eavesdropped word, words more intense and fearful as three o'clock came and went. Near four, he uncorked the bottle and took his first sip, disquiet inching toward panic as he waited on the cool slab of the old stone steps.

The afternoon distilled itself toward evening, the light growing richer, redder as he slowly consumed the wine. There was a murmuring in the town, an uneasy undertone. He went into the Quatre Chats, sat down, ordered.

Were they looking at him? Was it contempt in their eyes as they achieved some private sense of what was likely shared between the young American and the lamed engineer? But no, it was discomfort. A vague sympathy? As he lifted the glass to his lips, he felt his hand shake, the raw wine of the Quatre Chats cool on his tongue, noting the expression, sweet and bewildered, of the serving girl, Helene, sixteen and in love with Claude, eighteen and at the front, whom she wrote religiously, so people said, every night after the café closed.

At quarter to five, Rameau, her father, the man who owned the Quatre Chats, approached his table. He was short and verging to fat, but he stood before Morris with a terrible, respectful solemnity.

"Monsieur. Accompagnez-moi vous, s'il vous plaît?"

It came out as a question, but with the urgency of command, delivered with a dignity almost sacerdotal that brought Morris to his feet immediately.

They stepped out of the restaurant, those eyes upon them, workingmen's eyes full of an intimate loss. In the moment just before he reached the door, Morris thought he would faint as his heart slammed toward his throat and his stomach plummeted. It was something terrible, something not to be abided that had happened.

Rameau led him through the streets, down toward the

train yards in the peaceful afternoon. As they neared the station, the old man, who had not said a word there two paces ahead, suddenly fell back and softly took Morris's arm.

On the platform, Morris bit his lower lip almost all the way through, assuring himself it would not be so awful as it might be — another injury: a hand lost; a shoulder shattered. That would be all, some assault on wholeness, grisly perhaps, but bearable, something that did not touch the quick. But simultaneously, he felt his mouth falling, the corners bending downward hopelessly as some bundle of primitive nerves comprehended it was more horrible than his conscious mind — his optimistic, small-town American brain that still somehow believed in happiness, good fortune, and redemption — could admit.

They brought him back in the engine that towed his shattered train from where he died. He had volunteered to drive it. He had not been alone in that. They were brave, the lot of them, men behind the lines who perhaps courted danger all the more willingly for some guilt or jealousy of those who daily faced the guns. He had driven that engine through the countryside gradually more in thrall to war. The world resigned itself to a single gender, and then the old and the young were winnowed out, till white hair and the breaking voice vanished, and some unnatural regime of brothers was all that was left of civilization. Jean Baptiste had guided his train of food, of bullets, of medicine slowly down those tracks ripped and repaired four dozen times, inching over rails hardly ballasted at all, past blasted forest, poxed fields whose crops, one day, would grow ripe from the blood drunk by that earth. And on.

Till the unanticipated moment. The moment always potential: the accident, the lucky blow, the stroke some blond Hanoverian who probably looked something like Morris had no way to predict as he wound the giant gun around and let the projectile fly in the blind, imitative, and opposite metaphor of love. And why ought it have flown true? Why, though it did not strike either engine or track, should its shrapnel have pierced the boiler, which — confused, never meant for such an unexpected interruption of pressure — blew all its tubes and pipes? And why was the fireman climbing back in the tender to force the coal that had perversely jammed in that precise moment, the moment Jean Baptiste leaned forward to check a dial, adjust a valve?

It melted him. Morris had never seen anything like it, not even at Belleau Wood. The explosion spewed a hail of metal in a hellish wet out of the ruptured boiler; transformed the face and chest of the engineer into some kind of human pudding: a featureless, unrecognizable mass; eyes, nose, cheeks, chest, suddenly unreal, undefinable, some formless parody of flesh. Morris reeled back, apples and sour wine in his throat. There could be no identifying that remnant of a man as the one whose gaze had first ensnared him, whose mouth had met his own, across whose breast he had laid his head in sleep.

It was by his hands he knew him. Rough and stubby hands that had wrestled him to giggles that first night ("Whistle! Whistle!"), had cracked his cheek there beside the brook, and later, time after time, had gently driven him toward frenzy and release, then soothed his sweat-slick exhaustion till it all began again.

Other engineers lifted the corpse off the iron floor of the locomotive that had flown to the rescue and dragged the ill-fated supplies back to Varennes Ste. Claire for yet another journey tomorrow. A journey perhaps with that fireman miraculously saved, but without Jean Baptiste. Without the runaway from Perpignan who had matured much too fast in Marseilles, and had passed such lessons as he could along to a silly, crippled American soldier.

Morris stood over the body — the twisted, featureless body that he had loved and that had loved him — his face a mask of vacant grief: tearless, appalled.

He waited.

He waited until they came to take Jean Baptiste away, his scalded overalls grossly, absurdly bright in the train yard's glare. When they picked him up, when three men gathered arms and legs and stumbled the body into the back of a truck, Morris locked his jaw, set his mouth so hard to contain his despair that he broke a tooth, snapped the tip off an incisor for want of some other act that might vent the loss moiling hopelessly within him, so somehow it might not cool, congeal, and seal his heart as sure as stone.

Rameau, stolid Rameau, put his hand on Morris's shoulder.

It was thanks to Rameau that he ended the night in his own bed, in the ward of pentimentos between Lansdowne and Micheletti, stunned and awake.

◆   ◆   ◆

Awake.

How often, of late, you had lain in darkness, and how now you wished for sleep, your labors done. But, willing your senses wary, you could at best doze a bit.

It had taken too long, all of it. Such trouble, such efforts of dissembling as to leave even you, J. Skikey, masquer *extraordinaire*, exhausted. These complicated pleasures came at exorbitant cost: suggestive dialogues in the garden, the constant dullness of Justus Bechner, dependence for safety on a nattering boy as, day to day, the risk of capture increased. All for this night, the one repellent act that made your plan complete.

You had known this evening's supper would be your last in Christina. A voice within you spoke it. Your final opportunity shimmered after the stroke of twelve, and even as you crept toward resolution, you could not be certain of success. How carefully you had prepared the ground for this project: fertilizing with kindness, nurturing with smiles, warming with compliments, watering with compassion. There had been the gifts, the poetry, the folded notes left here and there throughout the house, the soulful looks you painted on your face. How skillful your simulation of emotion.

These were the tools, necessary as pliers, matches, needles in that other world, the items essential to realize your desires. You could only hope the rewards of your efforts were as sweet as you imagined.

To achieve what you wished, you had had to trust Sammy Pearlman. Only to a point, of course, but even that was enough to fan your nervousness. He had believed your lies of unscrupulous business partners, of an affair with one of their wives, and had agreed to monitor the telegrams from Kansas City as he was able. You had baited the arrangement with fifty dollars and the promise of more for his magazine enterprise, assuring him that, even if you had to leave, he would find the necessary sum behind the loose brick of the abandoned incinerator in the alley. There, too, he would leave any urgent message, signaled by a nosegay on the fence across the street, opposite your window. You had resisted the complexity of it, but the boy was enchanted, and so you humored him. Sullen, he was useless to you.

"Hell, Jay," he had said the day before, "why don't you clear out now?"

You mouthed the rehearsed excuse, baldly silly but cued to sixteen-year-old comprehension: honor and a new start and possible vindication. And instincts. The true reasons for your remaining were too refined for mortal understanding: would challenge the wisdom of angels themselves.

But you feared now — there in the darkness of your room, your tasks complete — that you had overreached. Too much depended on mere good fortune. Tomorrow you would go regardless of signals. It was done. You had attained all you wished here, satisfied your pride; your one regret that you would be able only to imagine the suffering you had caused. That was assumed from the beginning. How you wished now you might close your eyes to dream the first of many dreams of the blight you had unleashed on these shattered lives already beyond hope or redemption.

But any slumber deep enough for such visions might last too long, and you might open your eyes to guns and the cocky loudness of the law. All you could allow was that bright half sleep, rising over you like a bubble to burst in sudden wakefulness. And that strained you yet more, for it tweaked your memory — as if you had engineered it yourself in the cellar of the Four Deuces — at that point of your life more excruciating than all the rest.

Awake.

You were suddenly, terribly awake. You were on the floor, naked, sticky with blood in the darkness. At first you did not move. You lay utterly still, unwilling to risk the shift of some possible fracture, some organ unhinged. But slowly, pain seeped regardless through your body, and you recalled what had happened.

The room took shape before you in the light nearly imperceptible that filtered through the windows. You moved your head to look, tearing a bloody crust from the floor that adhered to your cheek. You found the shape of the table, the back door, Phelan's bed. Then your hearing returned, at least partially, a faint ringing in your ears. Phelan was snoring, the dark shape of him thrown across his mattress. Your own respiration clotted in your nose and throat, air whinnying in and out of your lungs, labored and hurt. You pulled yourself to your hands and knees, tears starting from your eyes at the throbbing of your bruised face, your stomach, the battered back of you torn and strained. You crawled toward your pallet; rest, your first thought.

But you were oddly too alert for that, and the snoring, first perceived only as proof of your senses, now reverberated inside your head. It was as if Phelan spoke. You listened, and in the growling heard his fury of hours — or was it moments? — before, his insults, what you had suffered.

You understood what had been done to you unwilling was unspeakable, not to be abided, but it was not the act itself that in that moment appalled you. It was its agent. If the home you had fled what seemed decades before had taught you of women's perfidy, you felt now doubly deceived by that of men.

Phelan's snoring echoed to where you knelt on the floor, echoed down within you to some age-old anger, some need too bloody to be understood. You rocked backward over your toes, the balls of your feet. Your heels touched ground, and you stood.

You stood naked in the darkness. Phelan slept. The embers glowed vaguely in the stove. Every part of you ached, but you spread your arms wide, taking your breath deep inside, taking in all vengeance, all fury, so you might act. From the slums hard by the junkyard, from the mansions along the North Shore, from the Loop, from the speakeasies salted amidst them all, from the other side of Division Street where the Italians whom you hated and who were now to be your allies lived and died: from all of these you sucked in the wind of rage. You, violated and betrayed.

Violator. Traitor. You glided down the stairs, breaths shallow and silent, a shudder moving through you despite your will. You, a ghost in that house which, in the black, might be any one in any moment of your life. Like some boy before the prospect of a cousin, sister sleeping in the next room, you advanced unsure of your reception.

How you had worked, how you had fought your own repugnance at this woman filled with gall. What did she know of bitterness? Yet, you had listened patiently as her life was laid before you, that litany of servitude, of men pained or blessed or both at once who thoughtlessly imposed their whims upon her. And she acceded. Hers was a story of torment quotidian and dull she had willingly endured, and you — master of the dark arts, moving now, half naked, toward the realization of your plans —

you wondered how she waited for you, if she had found the note you had slipped beneath her saucer: "I will come for you tonight."

Copied from the cheapest romance, like the flowers and those other tokens of courtship scattered over the last two weeks. Yet, fair warning too, and if she would not have you, all she need do was throw the bolt on her door. You coiled around the landing. How exquisite this desire, how sublime its realization: you descending through the black, plunging toward her in the night, the dark mirror of someone you might once have known.

At the base of the stairs, you were not sure if you could do it. She repelled you: her bearing, her voice, her body. All voluptuousness had been stolen there, or perhaps it had never been there at all. Too tall, too thin, too clumsy; too lost to housedresses and dusters, to routine and labor and the absence of attention. But, for you, had it ever been about voluptuousness at all? Only in the cellar had passion pounded in your veins. All other times, it was mere physiology.

You touched the doorknob; twisted. It moved beneath your hand. It was now, as you had planned it. You closed your eyes and spoke her name — or was it hers? — across the darkness, and she replied.

You slid toward her. Drapes drawn, high ceiling lost above you, its walls invisible, the room might have been some infinite pit. Fingers found you in the night, and a voice whispered: "Jay. My Jay. My Jay."

Breathless. Hardly audible at all, the sound of that name not yours lingering, as if it might be the initial sound of a hundred names: Jacob, Johnny, Joseph. You felt your muscles tighten, sealing you, turning you to something cold and bright. You slipped forward toward the mattress, squeezing your eyes shut, drawing from memory the one moment that you knew would drive you to fulfillment.

It hung through a roundheaded screw by the icebox, right beside the back door. In the vague light, it glistened as you pulled it forth, eight inches of tempered steel. What you and Phelan used when the iceman came; when there had been a melt and a new freeze outside.

You fondled it. All of it: the round ball of its handle; the tapering shaft that warmed with your touch. The snoring continued: the sound of repose, of satisfaction, of affection offered meaninglessly and of deception rewarded.

It would not be rewarded. You held the instrument in your hand and walked slowly, erect, across the room. You stood over the bed of the man who had saved you. Saved you only to betray you, to work his will of disappointed lust — disappointed by your own lacking for a woman you had never seen and would never see again — as if, for him, whatever bond had tied the two of you were substanceless as smoke. Your eyes adjusted now, hypersensitized as a cat's by your rage and loss. You looked down upon him.

You would never trust anyone again in your life.

You scanned his body, harking back to your bookish past, those medical texts bought only to fill the shelves of the parlor. Better not the heart, the thrust below the breastbone, for who knew, despite his gregariousness, if this man possessed a heart? Better the brain, the brain where dreams of desire were hatched, where the details of betrayal could be arranged so a child might end ravaged on a pine-planked floor. Between those green eyes, past the seat of highest thought, on through the head to where the more primitive of visions live, back to the very core of our animal selves.

So you stood. Raised the ice pick high into the air. Then, with all the force your young and so recently strengthened body possessed, you brought it down . . .

The remembered shock in your hands and arms of that steely thrust shot through you, and you exploded into release. Beneath you that dark shape whispered, ever more frantic, the ghost name yours not yours. Even as you collapsed, after such effort falling in upon yourself, you felt the frenzied grasping that told you you had conquered her. Phelan had saved her. Otherwise on that bed, you would have killed her, your passions too terrible to be endured. You felt the wetness of blood on your groin, touched it, and heard her soft weeping. She had struggled in her pain, your shoulder tender now from where her teeth had bored a mark you would not lose for days.

As you felt her body loosen beneath you in who knew what emotion — satisfaction, glory, shame — you bathed in the pleasure of the task complete, and of the hope your seed had sprouted. Then all your efforts would be thrice rewarded, your passage marked not only in mind and spirit but in flesh itself.

You pulled away. Your victory achieved, you wished nothing more than to be gone. She held on, whispering endearment, insisting on your presence. You reassured her, tamping a rising panic, willing yourself the ardent Romeo who nonetheless has admitted the lark. As you stood, she pressed a piece of paper into your hand.

"Please," she whispered, "please."

You took it, then plunged one last time over her, your mouth unwilling seeking hers, your fingers wadding the message — some affirmation of her love — and dropping it over the headboard to nestle with whatever dust might elude her there beneath the bed, so in the future she might find it, one more token of your loathing. You yourself needed no such talisman of your success.

You drew away, fading back into the darkness, out the door. In the pitchy hallway, naked, your clothes held in your hands, you flushed with the warmth of triumph, though still you were cautious, taught by your own experience to anticipate the unexpected.

When Phelan was dead — and you made sure, roiling that steel back and forth, hearing the fine crack of bone and that vaguer slough of tissue pierced and torn — you stood away, awash with numb relief. As before, you did not know what time elapsed. Perhaps it was mere seconds, perhaps hours. But dawn had not yet come.

Softly into your trance of vengeance complete, softly through that room, across the corpse there on the bed, there came a sound. And again. You shook your head. A knocking. Rap-rap rapping. And a voice.

"Phelan?"

Not too loud. Not an angry voice.

"Phelan?" Tap. "It's me. Phelan!"

A drunken voice. A woman's. Slowly you placed it. Sally's voice.

"Phelan?"

Phelan was dead in front of you, a hole drilled in his forehead, staring three-eyed toward the ceiling, toward the treasures that resided on the floor above, and on toward whatever Heaven shone above Chicago.

"Open up."

Sally had come back, had taken pity on the man who had found a fairy in an abandoned Chevrolet; who had stood with his cock slung out of his pants as she fled his house with a mouth full of curses. She had come back now to accede to desires that would never more be present in this world. You stood dumb, naked, covered with blood — yours and Phelan's — and knew suddenly what had to be done. You walked across the room, around the end of the counter, to the door.

"Huh?" you whispered through the crack.

"Phelan?"

"Huh?"

"Phelan? It's Sally."

Through the wood, splintery, warped, you could imagine her Polish blondness on the porch, still in the same dress, a whore past her prime, the face and breasts that had tried to possess you, the crotch with which dead Phelan had thought to make you a man.

"Get lost!" you rasped.

"Phelan!"

"Get lost!" You ravaged your throat much as you were able, no hard feat after beating, rape, and murder. "Get lost. I don't wanna see you around."

"Phelan!" It had a pathos to it, a whining sorrow. Yet behind you was a corpse. You kicked the door hard. "Get lost, bitch!"

The last words threatened to rise to those of a man with his voice intact. She began to cry, but soon after you heard her departing steps. You crept to the sink; dragged a wet towel hard across your face, your arms, your chest. You found your clothes, then returned to the bed. You were not sure you could move him.

When you opened the door, Wanda began to bark, but you calmed her with the whistle you had learned, the odd, throaty warble you heard the night that Phelan saved you. She quieted, whimpered as you dragged the body from the house, off the back stoop, through the junkyard. She accompanied you whining to the back, to the pyre where tires and lousy clothes and rotten shoes and who knew what emblems of joy — wedding dresses and spent rubbers and literary manuscripts, long desired carpets, drapes, sofas, tables — all had vanished into cinders. You grabbed the rake, and pulled away the coat of ash to reveal the coals aglow beneath.

You scrounged then for wood, dragged newel posts and chairs into the heap, settling Phelan comfortably upon them though the heat warmed the soles of your shoes and began to melt your eyebrows. You went back to the stoop, Wanda tagging at your heels, and grabbed the can of kerosene. You soaked two old sheets you found and cast them over Phelan, whose first name you had never known. You dashed back as the cloth ignited and the flames blew wild into the early morning black.

Back inside, you forced the cashbox under the counter and took every penny, then walked the few blocks to Lake Shore Drive just as the sky began to pearl. You found a taxi, and asked to be taken to Wabash Avenue. Number 2222.

In your room, sponged clean, nearly dressed, you wished that here it were that easy, that there were no need to wait till morning. You recalled the schedules Morris Farrell had sung; the whistles you yourself had heard in the early hours. All that remained now was the wait before leaving.

You would leave as well those cards, with the name you had taken and now lost, that for so long you had yearned to use. A month, no more, it had been yours, taken from you by a curious undertaker. You set one of them, so elegantly printed, in the middle of the bureau, under the mirror, and squinted at your dark reflection, bidding good-bye to what they had christened you in New York, there after Dion O'Banion was dead, where you first told the story of Phelan's murder.

Not exactly, of course, not what you had suffered, what Phelan had done to you, nor how you disposed of the body. That had been discovered soon enough, though not till you were safe in the realm of the South Side gang. But in New York, at a speakeasy on Broome Street, in the midst of one of those conversations that mix gangster and writer, gangster and actress, gangster and financier thrill seeker all together at one table, you transformed Phelan into a physician named O'Rourke, behind in his debts, who had invited violence by pulling a gun.

Your Brooklyn friends looked askance, but the brash young businessman was intrigued, and even more his shiny, careless wife, white as a flower with a laugh like gold. So you continued, smiling at your audience's curiosity, explaining how you had talked the Irishman out of trouble, offered him whiskey, gotten him drunk, taken him home, and slaughtered him with a letter opener. Then, to give more luster to your reputation, you made Sally an honest woman, the wife, in fact, of the respectable doctor. She knocked on the library door after the deed was done, asking if everything were all right. Then you — imitating the dead man — assured her through the lock that everything was fine, that she should go to bed.

One of them, one of the men from Brooklyn, a suave Neapolitan — doubtless a child of immigrants hungry for the merest survival; one who had worked as hard as you to achieve the suit and spats and demeanor of a man accustomed to the best life offered — the suave Neapolitan of the Five Points Gang looked across the table and said: "Ah, Gianni Schicchi."

"Pardon?" you said.

"Gianni Schicchi. Puccini's *Trittico*. The season at the Metropolitan a few years ago. You know the story. From Dante."

You agreed you did, sipping your whiskey, encouraging the talk that wandered toward Chaliapin and Catalani.

Next day, at the library, you checked out the *Divine Comedy,* and there discovered the story of your Florentine soul mate.

VII

I'VE GOT to be honest. I wasn't there. If it'd been night-time, or Sunday, well then, I'd've been an eyewitness. But it didn't work out that way, since they came in the morning on a Saturday and I'm a working man. What I know is what was in the papers, of course, and what I got out of Paul Beckner and his people, and what Edna and Morris had to say.

By the time all those telegrams went back and forth, the Sheriff and those fellows up in Kansas City both had a pretty good idea of who Jay Skikey was. But they told Paul — the G-men that is — they told Paul to sit tight, that they had to do some more checking. It was glory hounding. They should have reported it to their office in the capital — they got one over there — and either they'd've sent an agent over or told Beckner to go ahead and nab him. Seems like those boys up there were hell-bent for leather to get noticed by Mr. Hoover in Washington, so they go on playing the thing real close to their chests.

Comes that morning, and Paul gets a telegram telling him these two Federals are arriving on the *Belle*. I suppose you can put some of the blame on the Sheriff. The G-men said he ought to have had somebody watching the house. But hell, Paul only had two deputies — Aaron and Henry — and one was part-time, and besides, what do we know in this town about gangsters and how they operate? And the damn telegram didn't make it down here till two hours before the *Belle* pulled in, can you imagine? Six-thirty in the morning. They were all but here. Henry had to wake Paul up when he got it.

It was funny that morning, thinking back on it. When I got up, when I first woke up, Jay was in the bathroom. I heard him, shaving, I guess, humming to himself. Now usually I was the first one in there, especially Saturdays. Makes me wonder if he'd heard somehow, that early.

There he was singing away. He either didn't have a care in the world or he was so cool in a spot it didn't bother him. He came out and smiled at me, and later I saw him way out in the back, taking in the morning, I guess. We had breakfast and he was nice as ever — only read the sections of the paper after I was done and talked to Edna and all.

So, I get up and get my things and get myself off to the courthouse. I kind of liked that weekend work, the whole town so sweet and peaceful. I remember it was one of those late spring mornings we get here in June. Christina's famous for them, cool with lots of dew and prettier than sin. The ice wagon was going by, and somebody'd left a bouquet on the gate across the street for the Frimler girl. She had beaus and beaus, and it looked like one of them had probably raided Mrs. Pike's rosebushes the night before. Three just perfect red roses. I was going to kid her about it, I remember — oh, she was a sweet thing — but then I forgot on account of all that happened.

Anyway, I left, and everything I'm telling you now is what I heard. Seems the *Belle* pulled in right on time, and off hop those two hotshots from Kansas City, raring to make the papers. Paul didn't like them at all: smarty-pants boys who kept making fun of the place and took to telling him and Henry and Aaron what they should do and should've done. They go back in the freight agent's office for a few minutes to plan things out, and then they all get in Aaron's car since it was a good little roadster — a Ford, mind, but he kept it running like a top, I admit, even though I'm partial to Buicks — and off they went to the Farrells'.

To show you the kind of fellows those G-men were: they make Aaron park way down the block, and then they order — there's no other word for it — order him and Henry and Paul to surround the house, go around in other people's backyards and all, while they go in to arrest old Jay. Hell, Paul would have walked up to the door. The way it was, half a dozen people told me later they'd seen the G-men trying to look smooth as you please, and wondering who on God's green earth they were and what they were up to. Henry, when he was sneaking through backyards, he had to shush Mrs. Pike when she caught him. She was standing out on her back porch and she told me herself, she said: "Henry Potter, what're you doing slinking through here like some apple-snatching twelve-year-old at nine o'clock in the morning?"

Well, he looked at her cross and kept going, and she thought it was about the funniest thing she'd ever seen. She's not a bad lady, really, Mrs. Pike, even if she does teach piano.

Anyhow, the two G-men get up to the house, and then, instead of using the gate, they jump the fence. Jump it and land running and, quick as a whistle, they're up the steps and through the front door. Mrs. Frimler saw it out her parlor window, there with her tea for a little peace and — Bang! — there's these fellows attacking the house across the street. They've got their guns out and it's lucky Edna hadn't locked the door because they'd've broke it down for sure.

What happened then I'm not too clear on, because I had to get it from Edna and she was real upset about it all and then, of course, she took off. I guess they busted in with their pistols shoved out and there she was in the dining room in her duster. Poor old Edna. When she cleaned house she'd put on any old thing and tie her hair up. I mean, it is funny, sort of. This lady looking like the end of the world with a polishing rag in her hand and all of a sudden here are two gents in three-piece suits slamming into her house and shouting and waving guns around.

She screamed. She screamed to beat the band. Paul and Henry and Aaron heard it. Mrs. Pike and Mrs. Frimler and all the other neighbors. She even woke Morris up. Meantime, those two G-men were all over the place, running upstairs and kicking open doors and yelling and well, you'll pardon, but all hell broke loose. And in the middle of it, out comes Morris in only half his pants and Edna's caterwauling like it's Judgment Day and Mrs. Frimler's run out to get her collie and comes barreling over with the dog a barking fool 'cause she's going to save her neighbors from whatever the hell's going on.

Excuse me, if you have to. I mean, I don't know whether

it's civil to laugh about it, with all that happened afterwards. But I get tickled. Every time I think about it I get tickled.

So . . . Well, the so of it all is that there's no Jay. They busted into his room finally, and there are his trunks and an umbrella and one of his cards, set right there on the bureau:

J. SKIKEY
PROFESSOR OF AESTHETICS
AND ELOCUTION

Nothing else. It turns out — they forced the locks, you know — turns out the trunks were half empty. Down at the P.O., they remembered over the past two weeks Jay'd sent a couple packages to Chicago and one to New Orleans and another one to either Los Angeles or someplace else in California. They couldn't really recollect. Now, he'd left behind some nice stuff. A couple fine suits, for one thing. But that case of his, the one he had the night he first came, that was gone. He probably had his guns in there.

Well, by that time, of course, the Sheriff and the deputies had come on up and half the neighborhood was over and Edna was crying and Morris was white as a sheet. Those G-men were cursing like sailors. Mrs. Pike told me she had never heard such language and even Aaron said he didn't know half those words but you could tell they were dirty, just awful blue talk because they hadn't caught Jay Skikey. They were all set to go out and comb the woods and find him, and then Paul says: "What time did Skikey go out this morning, Edna? When's the last time you seen him?"

I guess she was still crying and crying. But she says finally:

"About eight o'clock. After Justus left. He had an early appointment, he said."

So Paul says to Morris: "Morris, when's that northbound freight through? About what time?"

And Morris says: "The eight-nineteen?"

"That's it. It's up past the Junction by now, isn't it?"

"Lord, yes," Morris says. "It pulls off at the Junction to let the *Belle* go by."

Paul got his dig in at those G-men, see? But quiet. Paul's not swelled up like they were. Well, they get all gathered up because they've got to send telegrams all over God's half acre and nail Jay Skikey someplace else close by. But Paul told me, he did, that he knew then there was no chance, that Jay'd smelled them out and that he'd got away.

He did. They've never caught him yet. We figure he went north and then doubled back, maybe headed to Texas. Hell, who knows? He could've gone East or off to California or up to Denver. Lordy, by now he could be in Paris or South America.

You know, if they'd let Paul Beckner handle it, maybe they'd've caught old Jay. We like to think that here, anyway. But he was probably smarter than any of us. He was one smart character, Jay Skikey. One slick, smart fellow, no doubt about that.

◆　　◆　　◆

Jay Skikey was a gangster.

Watering the garden as on any afternoon, Morris turned the statement over in his mind. He had pondered the notion the entire day, from the moment he was rousted out of bed by the craziest commotion he had confronted since the War.

His thoughts had not much clarified themselves. It was not Jay's lawlessness. Lawlessness held no particular horror for Morris. After seeing what lawful nations, governments, armies indulged in, he had no elevated expectations of individuals. Too, with his own past, he had limited patience with arbitrary distinctions of good and evil.

Still, from the first moment he heard, Morris had felt a peculiar disquiet, and it remained with him now as he filled the watering can yet again and returned to the tomatoes and beans. He queried all his readings of each individual moment with Jay Skikey, refracting it through his own loss, those dream-desirings turned to smoke by Jay's departure. Disappointment itself was bearable. Morris was no stranger to catastrophe, and one more disillusion should have no serious effect. Yet he was suspicious that there was something more, questions yet unformed nesting at the base of his brain. He knew he was a wounded man, and someone of Jay's sensibility would recognize that. If Jay had played with him as casually as an animal with his prey, what other games had he devised?

Out of the corner of his eye, Morris saw a figure in the alley. He set down the watering can and walked to the fence. It was Sammy Pearlman.

"Hey!" Morris said.

Sammy looked up, startled, and Morris was sorry to have spoken.

"What're you nosing around for?"

"Nothing," Sammy said too fast. "Nothing. What's it to you?"

Morris shrugged. "It's the alley next to my backyard, I guess. You lose something?"

"What's it to you?" Sammy snapped again.

"Like I said, my backyard." He remembered that Jay had spoken of the boy, that Justus had remarked on the time the two of them spent together. "Jay's gone, you know."

Sammy's eyes flickered, simultaneously bereaved and furious, before he regained himself.

"Yeah. Yeah. So?"

"Nothing." Morris turned back to the garden. "Nothing. That's all."

"He owed me money," Sammy blurted suddenly.

Morris glanced at him perplexed; amused. "Oh, really? You figure he might've dropped some back there when he made his getaway?"

Sammy stood, sneering and defiant, and yet, in his very bearing, Morris sensed a fear, and a great disillusion.

"How much?"

For an instant, something passed across Sammy's face, a sad cloud of boyish defeat, as if he were on the edge of a confidence. "None of your business!" He wheeled suddenly. "It was between him and me. I guess I'm the chump, that's all."

He stalked away, his steps heavy on the cinders. Morris followed the retreating figure with his eyes, wondering if he were watching the disappointment of Jay Skikey's accomplice. Perhaps Sammy had somehow warned Jay of the G-men's arrival, thrown rocks at his window or left some hidden message. Had Jay promised him money to win his assistance, funds for a train ticket or a new suit of clothes? Had it been only money he promised Sammy Pearlman?

He smiled at the speculation, at the twinge of jealousy that tweaked him. The idea was as fantastic as his own desires had been. Realistically, he told himself, gangsters — even those from Chicago who had drunk champagne with Al Capone in those happy years before the Crash — would be unlikely to understand Morris Farrell and the flame he still carried for a French engineer. He ought to leave off his mooning. Jay Skikey had come momentarily and reminded him of the depth of his loss, had helped him confront that loss, and had gone when that obligation was met, as ghostly an agent as Carmichael and Jean Baptiste at the gorge and the curve there on his nightly rounds.

He set the watering can next to the back stoop and went inside, where he found Edna crying again. Her tears had erupted sporadically since the fright that morning. She had wept at the shock of the assault, the revelation of Jay Skikey's real identity; the shambles the G-men had left his room in upstairs. She had sniffled as they questioned her; as Paul Beckner tried to comfort her while the detectives worked to get more out of Morris than he was willing to offer. She had erupted again when Justus arrived on an early lunch hour, beside himself for having missed the excitement. Through the afternoon, as Morris tried with small success to resume his interrupted sleep, he had heard her from time to time, soft sobbings of hurt, though for the G-men, the house, for unwittingly harboring a gangster, or for Jay Skikey himself, Morris did not know.

She was at the sink, methodically stringing beans in the colander, snapping the ends and stripping the veins in one smooth motion as she hiccoughed her fathomless emotion. Morris stood in the doorway, arms at his sides, unsure. He realized in that instant the terrible distance between them, the distance he himself had done most to create in his self-imposed solitude, in his terror of intimacy that made him push away even his own blood.

He did not know what to do.

She glanced at him, and suddenly her flood of tears was worse. She left the beans and stood before him, her fingers over her eyes, racked now with crying, her entire, long body given over to shuddering, terrible grief. Morris recalled that need he had had once for that overwhelming release he could not indulge the day Jean Baptiste was killed, the day he instead snapped that tooth.

Before him, very slowly, she crumpled, her arms crossed over her middle. Clumsily, he lurched to catch her. She collapsed against him, and, holding her, he wondered how long it had been since he had touched her.

"Edna. Edna," he said mechanically, stroking her hair. She did not stop, her weeping climbing now toward hysteria. He held her tighter. "Edna. It's all right, Edna."

He felt a terrible closeness, and regret, realizing all those years he had offered this lonely woman no kindness, no companionship, none of the sympathy and sustenance that ought to be natural to siblings. Sharing a roof, eating the food she faithfully prepared day to day, leaving to her the realities of making beds and paying bills and putting together what little security they could muster, and yet he knew nothing of her heart.

He heard Justus come through the front door, and looked at him helplessly, guiltily, as he burst into the kitchen. Justus's eyes accused him across the room, but all he said was "Come on, Morris. Come on. Let's get her to bed."

They half-carried her to that back parlor where she slept and laid her down. Justus sent him to crack some ice and, after he had brought it, across the street for Mrs. Frimler.

"Should I get the doctor?" Morris asked timidly.

Edna threw herself upright. "No doctors! No doctors!" she demanded, her voice ragged with hysteria, "No doctors!" There was a new barrage of sobs.

Justus looked Morris in the eye and jerked his head once to send him for Mrs. Frimler, massaging the ice on Edna's temples. Morris's request was half inchoate, but his neighbor followed him, full of prematurely gray efficiency, tossing both the men out of Edna's bedroom and, after the patient finally fell asleep, ferrying some leftovers from across the street to feed Morris and Justus, leaving them with strict instructions to call her if there were any problems in the night.

Over the table, Justus quizzed Morris for details of the day's events. After they rinsed the dishes, Justus retreated upstairs, and Morris — late for perhaps the first time since he had first walked track years before — rushed for the door. As he left, he noted on the sideboard that copy of the *Inferno* that Callan had brought for Jay Skikey.

And he resolved, when he returned that night, to take it back to his room, along with that translation with the Doré illustrations high on the shelves of the parlor, to search, canto to canto, for the Italian Callan McAlpern had thrown with such triumphant meanness across the table the night of that supper that now seemed as long lost as France.

She was upset. There's no denying that. Now, she had every right to be. Soon as I heard about things and I could take my lunch, I hightailed it down to the Farrells' to see what in damnation was going on. They'd busted my door. I always left it locked. Not that I had anything to hide. But it seemed to me, living with strangers around, next door to people like Jay Skikey turned out to be, well, it seemed like a good idea, don't you think?

Like I said, Edna was upset. Those boys from Kansas City were pretty unhappy they'd missed old Jay, that he'd skipped out on them, and they messed things up good, even cut his mattress open to see if he'd hidden something inside. No wonder she was shaky. I did what I could for her, but I had to get back to work. Well, she wasn't any better off when I got there that night. Morris was trying to help her out, but what did Morris know about that kind of thing? She was weeping and moaning, and I sent him over to get Mrs. Frimler — women always know better what to do at times like that — and got Morris out of there and made sure he got to work. Somebody had to be responsible for things, you know.

It seemed funny to me. Peculiar, I mean. Sure, she's going to be plenty scared. Good Lord, with all that had happened, and realizing she'd had a real, live gangster in the house. But Edna was no shrinking violet. All those years putting up with Morris, making the books balance, taking care of her daddy before he died. She was no silly girl, old Edna. But she was just a jelly bowl that night. And it didn't get much better.

I don't mean she didn't get ahold of herself. Sort of. Next day, breakfast was out same as always, and even if she didn't look too good, Edna was up and dressed. But something wasn't right. Not just that her eyes were red, not just the next day but every day after, like she'd been crying when she was by herself. For one thing, she wasn't keeping the house like usual. Not to say things were dirty, even messy. Maybe I was just on my guard for what had happened. But she hadn't dusted always, or a book that was off the shelf in the morning was still off the shelf in the afternoon. You understand, she usually kept things so spotless you noticed when something was out of place. More than anything, though, it was Edna herself. She walked funny and talked funny, and looked, well, kind of wounded. Hell, kind of like Morris. That whole week she wasn't quite there.

I tried to get her to talk, but she wouldn't. Sometimes she'd say: "It's such a shock, such a shock." And sometimes she'd say: "I'm very tired, Justus. Just tired." And finally it was like she didn't hear me. I sat Morris down one afternoon and tried to have a word with him about it. He wasn't much help, but you could tell by the way he looked at her at supper he was worried. Even he tried to buck her up. I mean, he was never mean to her before, but in those last few days he'd say more to her than usual. He even helped her pick the dishes up before he went to work, which was the first time that ever happened that I knew about.

None of it did much good, though. Couple nights, after I was in bed upstairs, I could hear her moving around, going from room to room. I'd hear the kitchen door squeak, and then, later, I'd hear her in the parlor — my room was just over the parlor. Back and forth, back and forth, like a dog in a strange place who can't figure out what to do.

Now, I have to face it straight and I know what you're thinking: that Edna's acting a whole lot like a spurned woman, a girl whose fellow's skipped out on her after he's gotten what he wanted. Maybe old Jay had. I don't deny it.

He was sure no angel, and he'd probably ruin a woman for the sheer devilment of it. Anyway, could you really blame Edna? What fun did she have in her life, I ask you, and if some slick fellow — "quality people," like she said — was sort of courting her one way or another, well, why shouldn't she want to give him what he asks for?

I'm not saying that's the way it necessarily was. All those ideas started coming up like clover after she took off. That was only a few days later. I'd heard her downstairs again. I didn't know then, but probably she was packing. Next morning, she looked a lot better — had her color back and even smiled a couple times. I said something about it over lunch down at the Greek's, that it seemed like Edna was finally getting over the shock of it all.

When I got home, I found Morris there in the kitchen. He was, well, you ever seen a steer when they're fixed to butcher it, when the fellow gets up over it and brains it? A kind of glazed look like every nerve's had its circuit blown. That's how Morris was. I guess he'd just found the note. Edna'd left it in the watering can, so he'd only come on it after she was good and gone.

She was nobody's fool. She caught the milk train north, the one through around ten. Mrs. Pike saw her leave. Said Edna had on one of her go-to-town dresses and a wicker laundry box. She was working in her flower beds and went down the walk to the gate and said to her, "Why, Edna, are you going on a trip?" And Edna gave her this kind of funny smile and said: "Oh, no. No. I'm taking a box of scraps down to the church for the quilting circle." The ladies down at the Baptist Church here, see, they get together once a week to make quilts for the charity cases.

Well, then, she walked downtown and over to the station and bought herself a ticket for Kansas City. Told the agent she'd had a letter from a cousin telling her her great-aunt was very poorly, and that she hoped she wouldn't get up there too late for anything but the funeral. The train pulled in and up she got and that's the last time anybody in Christina saw hide nor hair of her. Not a postcard or a letter in all the years, five years this past summer. She might as well've walked off the edge of the earth.

There was lots of talk — ugly, ugly talk — after she up and left about her and Jay and how they must've carried on, and people told stories — made up stories, if you ask me — about this and that: how they'd gone by the house such and such a day and heard noises and knocked and nobody came to the door. Well, you know what I think of that kind of jaw. When she was gone, some folks said that proved she had something to be ashamed of, and more than once I heard it said like there was no doubt about it that she'd found out she was . . . well, that she was carrying Jay Skikey's baby and went off to have that taken care of. It's possible, I guess, even though you'd think she could've come up with some excuse to go up the line a ways and gotten it done and come on back. But I guess Edna probably wouldn't've known about that kind of stuff.

There was another crowd who had it she'd helped Jay all along, and had run off to meet him someplace. I didn't have much truck with that either, even though Paul Beckner gave it some thought. If they had it all set up, I say, why'd she spend a whole week bellyaching after he left? Why not wait longer, so it didn't look so funny?

Some other folks said she'd taken off to see if she could

find Jay, that she'd fallen in love with him even if he was a gangster. Remember, we didn't know what a god-awful type he was till later. Edna wouldn't've known what she was getting herself into. I guess, of all the gossip that went around, I felt best about that idea, that she went looking for him. It puts old Edna in the best light, and she sure didn't deserve to be put in a bad one. Edna was a good, hard-working, Christian woman, and if she was in love with Jay Skikey, that's not her fault. It's just she might have made a better choice, don't you think?

◆　　◆　　◆

Through his head that evening, as he made his way down the switchback through the final dusk, the words spoke to him in the rustle of leaves; rasped in the crunch of his boots on the ballast. He wondered if this night his ghostly lovers might appear, to whisper sadly, mockingly, the explanation of the trembling Aretine:

> That goblin is Gianni Schicchi,
> who runs rabid, mangling us all.

It consumed him, the realization of his own deception. For the first time since Varennes Ste. Claire, he had revealed himself, if only subtly, to someone else. He realized now he had played the fool to a gangster who — for what dark reason who could fathom? — had played at seducing him as he seduced his sister.

All through the afternoon, the truth had gradually revealed itself. In the first hours after he woke, her absence did not strike him as strange. Often she was gone during the day: to buy groceries, mail a letter, on rare occasions to pay a visit. As the hour edged past three, however, a slight unease murmured through him, growing in volume as he waited longer, stunning him finally when he went outside to work in the garden, and found the note secreted in the watering can.

Dear Morris,
    I have to go now. I cannot explain. Please understand. I know Justus will help take care of you. The deed to the house is in the strongbox. There is money there to keep you for the next month. Do not hate me. I must do this. There is a broiler in the oven for supper. Turn it on at three-thirty.
                        Your sister,
                        Edna

The broiler was indeed there. She should have thought he would not find the note till after four. But she probably was not thinking. The pen had shaken as she wrote, he could see. Edna had a firm, almost masculine script, but this writing dipped and swirled like the practice of a new hand not fully mastered, or of a person experimenting with some corner of the soul — astounding, frightening — never before revealed. That, Morris understood better when he went to the strongbox.

Edna had put it back in its accustomed place, deep under her bed, and had left the key in the lock. Morris pulled the dust ruffle up from around the frame and dragged it out. The deed was there, and twenty-five dollars in cash. They had once had a bank account, but Edna had closed it after the Crash. Twenty-five dollars would serve till next payday, there was no doubt. Morris had no idea how much money Edna had taken with her.

He fingered the bills, her last gift to him, dumbfounded.

He had never imagined his sister might abandon him, though he had never paid her much attention, even before he had gone off to war. She had always been there regardless, and her departure now left him definitively alone, linked with nothing but spirits, those two men he had loved. And he did not know what to do.

As Morris shoved the box back far beneath the bed, something caught his eye. A wrinkled piece of paper nestled half hidden between the wall and one of the legs of the headboard. Straining beneath the springs, he caught it between his third and fourth fingers and drew it out.

It was only a half sheet, folded, then wadded up. And faintly stained. For a moment, he held it there in the rich, afternoon light, then slowly pulled it open. It was her stationery: a single rosebud in the right corner in gray, the very simple, almost painfully feminine pattern she bought year after year. He fingered the cheap paper: his sister's talisman, his sister gone.

My darling Jay . . .

His gut turned to water, and from his mouth came a cry short and hoarse as the birth of a sob.

Then he knew. He knew with the awful, clean searing of the end of self-delusion. In those few weeks, Edna had lived what he had only imagined. Hers had been no secret yearnings, rekindled by the set of a man's torso and dreamt of in late night darkness. Her desires had been physical, and realized. He turned the paper over, touched the brown tracings of the bloody fingers which had once held the note, the fingers of a man who had wheedled from Morris the timings of trains as easily, perhaps, as he had wheedled Edna's virginity.

Quel folletto . . .

That goblin. That cannibal minister of dread. Johnny Skikey. Gianni Schicchi. How he must have laughed, like those people who registered at hotels as Millard Fillmore or Pierre Beauregard. How he must have never counted on Callan, who would recognize him instantly, smell the fraud, but who was enough of a goblin himself — mysterious, perverse — not to make accusations outright, but to layer them with mean or cautious allusion. Why that night might he not have angrily cast down his accusation — he comes disguised! — instead of speaking it only in a foreign tongue? He could have exposed the trickster then and there, before the desires of sibling hearts converged unawares and shot one into flight and the other to pieces.

For Morris was mangled, sure as the minor damned in Dante, Johnny Skikey's teeth deep in his flesh, though Johnny Skikey be a hundred, a thousand miles away. He had done his work well, if not in Hell then in Christina. As Morris walked into the Junction that night, he felt a lightheadedness he could only compare with that of France, with the faintness that comes of loss of blood and pain beyond nerves' capacity to endure it.

He spoke even less than usual at Lloyd and Eddie's table, though as the southbound *Bonnie Blue* racketed past, he raised his head, his face quizzical, listening till the last clacks disappeared. He lapsed back to his coffee then, silent as before, and left soon after, Eddie and Lloyd later averred, with a funny, thoughtful look on his face, vanishing into the star-washed June, headed toward Christina.

He crossed the bridge, over the river's muddy trickling, thinking of Edna, thinking of Jay. And slowly, his bitterness dissipated, as he began to understand how he might make peace with his loss. At least, if only briefly, in that house there had been love, that house of boarders and boredom, of too little laughter and affections never voiced. He hoped, since Edna had gone, that she had gone seeking Jay, and that she might find him, and that the simple fact of her searching might somehow redeem that gangster, make him admire the honesty of desire, so, even if Morris's need had seemed to Jay some repugnant aberration, he still would see in the sister of that veteran, that trackwalker, the passion that abides in the human heart.

He came up out of the wash into the ravine, and felt Carmichael beside him, there not to judge but to accept, to place his arm over the shoulder of the man who had had to watch him die and give him comfort. He did not speak to him. Carmichael rarely did, his face that of serene resignation, as if he were perhaps not really sure what had happened to him, or why he had been assigned by some heavenly officer to haunt Morris Farrell, accepting the charge as his brief mortal incarnation as a soldier had taught him.

Carmichael faded as Morris left that ravine like a trench of the furious War that had first forced him to confront who he was. And having done so — first with Carmichael, then with Jean Baptiste — he had drawn back. Truth had offered itself, but in the face of those two deaths and his own dreads and the burden of what Christina had taught or not even mentioned as beyond all mentioning, he had sunk into himself and returned home to live a life not life at all, till a gangster came to release him again, and then sought finally not him but his sister. Earlier the sad irony of it would have moved him to tears, but now, with a terrible peace, he walked toward the arms of his lost lover who waited at the Horseshoe Curve.

Jean Baptiste greeted him: fresh as that first day, minus his limp, remade whole in the afterworld, murmuring words doubtless meaningful without need of translation in that land beyond death. He walked beside Morris, his hands shameless as they might be in a place of pure desiring. And as he soothed Morris — that onetime American soldier, that American soldier fourteen years gone, who had mourned the gruesome passing of a French engineer now half a life and world lost — the last of those wounds from the jaws of Jay Skikey were healed, and Morris Farrell was free to act.

It was not for Jay he did it. Not for Edna. Not for any sense of loss or betrayal. His ghosts had affirmed his worth, and that worth was in the realm of the spirit, where he should always have been, perhaps, and where he would go now for good.

The *Belle* pounded down out of Christina, out of the town that had been his since birth, whose growth he had watched as it had watched his, that had known him in both glory and ruin. The locomotive wailed through the night, maneuvering the switchback, roaring closer and closer, gathering speed, singing through the curve. Electric, peaceful, Morris watched it approach, the headlight shimmering down the rails. There it was: that point of desire, that hole in the darkness, beyond it the engine that cleft all before it.

He was no fool. He stood aside as he always did, till there could be no braking, till the headlight swelled in his face, till the train's straining energy filled the very air. Strangely, magically, he felt the same rush of wanting he had felt in that foxhole, in that afternoon in an abandoned shed near Varennes Ste. Claire, felt it more completely than memory can explain.

Suddenly, his arms spread wide, he stepped in front of the engine, embracing all he had ever desired, flying instantly shattered into the world of those he had most truly and faithfully loved.

◆   ◆   ◆

It smashed him to pieces. I had to go down to do the official identifying. I mean, we all knew who it was — the clothes were Morris's and you could sort of recognize him and, besides, who the hell else would be out there on the tracks that time of night? But I had to go down and look and sign the papers.

He was barely held together. The *Belle* comes barreling down out of here, and the trains always have trouble braking on that curve, and those are powerful locomotives. Nobody hit with one of those would have a Chinaman's chance. And old Morris sure didn't.

You can imagine the ruckus. The gossip gals had a field day: first Edna runs off, then Morris gets killed. There at first, the railroad was real anxious for everybody to know that Morris did it to himself. They were scared Edna'd show up again and try to collect a judgment. She didn't, of course. She probably to this day doesn't know what happened. Then, when they finally got Grace Mellors down here, she didn't seem too interested in going to court. She was too busy getting to know Christina and making plans with the house, and I imagine, as far as she was concerned, as long as she was sure she was getting the property, it didn't make much difference whether it was an accident or not.

I don't know. Maybe she figured from the first they were right, that Morris did kill himself. The engineer swore up and down and the fireman along with him that they saw Morris alongside the tracks like usual when all of a sudden he pitched in front of the train when it couldn't have been more than ten yards away. Spread his arms out, they said, like some damn bird. They braked down fast as they could — threw some people out of their berths, I guess, and a fellow in the kitchen knocked his head open and had to stay in Christina a few days after he got stitched up.

There was nothing they could do for Morris. He was probably dead before he hit the ground. Threw him I don't know how far. It took them a while to even find him. The engineer — fellow about Morris's age — said it was as bad as anything he saw in the War.

They picked up the pieces — I'm not being disrespectful, mind, it was almost that bad — and slung him up in the baggage car and headed on to the Junction. They left him with poor Lloyd and Eddie down there, the fellows Morris used to see every day, and finally in the morning they brought the body on up to Christina.

Callan did a good job on him. As good as you can do on a body mauled like that. We had a nice funeral. A fair number of people showed up and Willie Bills got the veterans together and them that still could wore their uniforms. They even got a bugler from the Boy Scouts to play taps. I did most of the planning, since Grace Mellors didn't even show up until the day before. It took that long for us to remember about that cousin up in Kansas City and find an address and get a telegram to her, and for her to get gathered up to come down.

Now, I don't have anything against Grace and I.J. They've always treated me nice. I just didn't like the way they hit town like a tornado and took over the house and booted me out without so much as a fare-thee-well. I'd lived there a good long time and I was about the best friend Morris and Edna had and it seemed to me I didn't get quite the treatment I deserved.

There was a while there where it was all anybody talked about, and a lot of people blamed Edna and, of course, Jay Skikey, Dandy Allan, whatever, and even a few of them said I should've looked out for Morris better or that Eddie and Lloyd should have kept a better eye on him that night. Can you imagine? You know, though, sometimes I kind of blame Callan McAlpern. He's one queer duck, and you'd have thought he might have minded his own business. If he hadn't been so snoopy, maybe old Jay would've stayed on and, who knows, things might have worked out for him and Edna.

Pretty silly, I guess. The leopard can't change his spots, and somebody like Jay Skikey, well, he'd've been up to some new devilment eventually. Poor old Jay. I'm not fooling. Somebody with that much bad to look back on, who's done that much meanness. Why, I bet he didn't want for Morris to die. How could he know? Some people, I guess, get to the point where everything they touch turns out ugly. Must be an awful burden, if you think about it. Like having the whole world on top of you.

There is one last thing. I never knew whether to credit it much, since Sal Watson himself said he couldn't be sure. I ran into him one day down at the Greek's, oh, it must've been over a year after everything happened. He'd set himself up in another rented room, at the McElroys' near the station. I'd got myself a little apartment by then, thanks.

Anyway, he's there with his case, clanking like usual with all those nuts and bolts, headed out on another one of those trips all over hell and gone. We get to talking, and he tells me he's been out to San Francisco, to some convention or other, and he's on Market Street, there with a couple of buddies on his way to lunch, when he looks across the street and there's this trolley car stopped.

And he says to me: "Now, Justus, I can't swear it because I didn't get a good enough look. But there was this lady standing on the back platform, and she sure could've passed for Edna Farrell. I can't be certain of it. But if that woman wasn't Edna then she could've been her twin."

I like to think it was, I guess. That it proves my theory. That Edna did fall in love with Jay Skikey, and, for one time in her life, decided to do what she wanted to do, that after he skipped out, she took off after him. It didn't matter that he was a gangster; that he was on the lam, just that he'd been good to her. Maybe people were right and she was carrying his baby, and she bore that baby and still she kept right on his tail. Or maybe she had a spinster aunt, and she left that baby with her, like happened to Jay Skikey once, so she could keep on looking for him.

But that part, the last part, I hope that isn't true.

Just like, for Edna's sake, I hope she never found him.

EPILOGUE

TUMBLING OUT of the mountains, east to west, the train fell like a star, as you, comfy in your Pullman, reviewed the brief career of J. Skikey, Professor of Aesthetics and Elocution, cast headlong from Chicago toward a small-town resort, there to rot for all time but for an undertaker's learning and your own ambitions.

And what glorious chaos you had left in your wake.

At best, she was pregnant, and would bring into the world another child with your eyes, your skin. A reminder ever present of your passage. How endless her regret, that woman confined to a drudge's life, and, too, her brother, who would ever more recall your insincere seduction by a throbbing watering can.

How utter your triumph as, year to year, day to day, their bitterness grew blacker, their despair more profound in that town that should have sheltered you. What vengeance you had achieved — on men, on women, on life itself — there in Christina, more so than in all those sessions when you exercised your arts in the basement of 2222 Wabash Avenue, for fury now was not just what you might wreak with pincers and lighted cigarettes. You had mastered the quintessence of the torturer's art — to flay not the doomed but those condemned to live.

If before you had caused pain, it was physical, and imposed on those who hurt you or had somehow betrayed either you or those to whom you owed allegiance. But now, you had discovered yours was a grander purpose; you, the man without history.

So, your name was not Johnny Skikey, Gianni Schicchi: minor, rabid trickster. No. The Trickster. Thrice Belial. Twice Beelzebub. Not October's child but the Father of Lies. Master Deceiver. Bringer of Dread.

There on a train in that vast desert of unbroken desolation, sweeping through darkness visible, you raised the shade. Face pressed to the glass, eyes bright on the future, you sought in the dawn's sky the star of your destiny.